MW01232756

An Agreeme... ...

Bareback by Chris Owen
Cowboy Up edited by Rob Knight
Deviations: Domination by Chris Owen and Jodi Payne
Deviations: Submission by Chris Owen and Jodi Payne
Don't Ask, Don't Tell by Sean Michael
Fireline by Tory Temple
Historical Obsessions by Julia Talbot
Jumping Into Things by Julia Talbot
Landing Into Things by Julia Talbot
Latigo by BA Tortuga
Locked and Loaded edited by SA Clements
Music and Metal by Mike Shade
Need by Sean Michael
Out of the Closet by Sean Michael
Perfect by Julia Talbot
Rain and Whiskey by BA Tortuga
Redemption's Ride by BA Tortuga
Shifting, Volumes I-III, edited by Rob Knight
Tempering by Sean Michael
Three Day Passes by Sean Michael
Tomb of the God King by Julia Talbot
Touching Evil by Rob Knight
Tripwire by Sean Michael
Tropical Depression by BA Tortuga
Under This Cowboy's Hat edited by Rob Knight

This is a work of fiction. Names, characters, places, and incidents either are the product of the author's imagination or are used fictitiously. Any resemblance to actual events, locales, organizations, or persons, living or dead, is entirely coincidental and beyond the intent of either the author or the publisher.

Redemption's Ride
TOP SHELF
An imprint of Torquere Press Publishers
PO Box 2545
Round Rock, TX 78680
Copyright © 2006, BA Tortuga
Cover illustration by Rose Meloche
Published with permission
ISBN: 1-934166-44-8, 978-1-934166-45-1
www.torquerepress.com

All rights reserved, which includes the right to reproduce this book or portions thereof in any form whatsoever except as provided by the U.S. Copyright Law. For information address Torquere Press.
First Torquere Press Printing: November 2006
Printed in the USA
If you purchased this book without a cover, you should be aware the this book is stolen property. It was reported as "unsold and destroyed" to the publisher, and neither the author nor the publisher has received any payment for this "stripped book".

Redemption's Ride
By BA Tortuga

Prologue

The pain he understood. The burning. The fear. The white-hot agony of the shattered bones in his arms. Even the mocking and the screams were familiar, almost a balm.

The smell was the thing.

The rope was covered in pitch, the mixture of sulfur and burning flesh and hair making his eyes roll as he snapped at the air, heart pounding furiously in his chest. They were laughing; he could hear them, laughing and watching, the rope going tighter and tighter around his throat, burning into his skin. His bloodied toes brushed the dust, his fingers caught behind him.

So long. He'd managed to run longer than anyone he'd know. This posse hunted like none other. He'd run, but they'd driven him into the ground, followed the trail he'd left without question. No one escaped judgment.

No one.

"I warned you, dog. Did I not tell you the punishment for the crimes you committed?" The voice settled in the base of his neck, something new within him screaming out in fear and sorrow. Part of him rejoiced. He'd hidden his prize away in the hills, buried deep upon land that burned his very skin, slowed him until he was prey.

He could see her, see her eyes in his mind, see her fear as her parents led her down the valley, toward the black smoke that billowed up into the sky. He'd known the punishment for what he'd done. The pain.

He'd known, but he'd done it anyway.

So part of him knew that he had won.

The rest of him was rage.

The rope pulled again, then again, and his eyes rolled, entire body fighting for breaths that he hadn't needed only days before.

"You were my most trusted, my most feared. I loved you more than any other, so you will suffer more than any other ever would have." He could feel the edges of those words inside him, tearing into him like knives. Glowing red eyes pinned him, stared down into his soul. His soul. What had he done to deserve that? "You have betrayed me. Betrayed your brothers."

There weren't no use to deny it. He had. He'd've done it again. The words were lies. Those eyes had never known love. Only hunger.

Another tug on the rope filled him with agony. "Beg me for death, Aquilon. Beg me."

Fuck that. He'd never begged, not even before he'd changed sides. He spit, as best he could, the tiny bit of wetness sizzling on the bastard's face.

Claws flashed out, splitting open his stolen clothes, his skin, the fire sharper than anything he'd ever felt, and he tried to cry out, the sound a mere gurgle, a bubble in a closing throat. The rope tugged again, his feet leaving the ground altogether, blood pounding in his head.

"Beg me and I will show you mercy. I will make a special place for you in Hell."

"L…liar." That he knew. They lied. They always had.

That smile grew, teeth like a rattlesnakes, sharp and dripping with a venom unlike any other. His bladder let loose and he shuddered, frozen right down to the bone. Hands landed on his shoulders, tugging him down into the burning pitch, then easing the pressure, allowing him the mixed blessing of one more breath, one more second. "Beg me, dog. Beg me, and I will kill you."

He shook his head and those eyes flared, staring into him. "Do you honestly believe for a moment that you will win, dog? That you can survive me? Survive your punishment?" Claws dug into his flesh, each one pushing through with a pop. "I will keep you like this for days, until there is nothing within you but pain and you will be on your knees, offering me anything for it to end. You will be nothing but meat."

Something nipped at his ankle and he kicked out, a pained yelp ringing through the air. Animals swarmed around his legs and he kept fighting, kept kicking and hurting, making each of them hurt in turn. The growls and snarls were music to him.

Music.

He knew music. His eyes rolled, the memory of a high, soft voice singing to him, soft fingers in his hair as he ran with her in his arms, ran from the black, oily smoke.

Amazing Grace, how sweet the sound. Sing with me now. What, you don't know the words? Didn't no one ever sing to you? That's awful sad. I'll teach you, Hawk. I will. Ma showed me real good. You reckon Ma's in Heaven, Hawk? You reckon I'll see her there? It goes I onced was lost, but now I'm found. Was blind, but now I see...

Something behind him moved, shifted and the rope jerked him up hard enough he snapped. He felt the skin in his throat pull and tear, then snap, the rope and pitch inside him. "No. No, you stupid bastards! You pulled too soon!"

The red eyes disappeared, howls and screams filling the air around him, fur and blood flying into the air as the crowd faded, disappeared, leaving him to swing. He could hear it, the creak and groan as his muscles jerked and danced, bouncing on the end of the rope.

Hawk – she called him Hawk – thought he saw something at the edge of the firelight, something still and strong, something watching him like he was a great puppet on a burning string.

The ground trembled as it came forward, hooves lashing at the fire that was growing around him.

Death was coming for him and he didn't have the breath to beg.

Chapter One

Damn, he was tired. Preacher sent his cheroot winging into the fire and took another sip from his cup. Little Bear was scrubbing the bean pot, and Abraham was already gone, sleeping the sleep of the newly righteous and farting his damned fool head off.

Maybe Preacher needed to get him a real church. This tent meeting thing reached a lot of folks, but it sure was hard on the ass, being in the saddle all day, and hard on the back, sleeping under a wagon.

Preacher sighed. Life was a damned sight easier before he got religion and left off the drinking and the bank robbing. Jett had set him on the road, passing on the tent and the Preacher hat, though, so he figured he had to keep moving until he found some young fool who needed redemption.

He got up and took his plate over to Little Bear, clapping the big man on one shoulder. "Good supper, Bear. Much thanks."

Bear just nodded, as he always did since he'd lost half his tongue to a gambler he owed money, and Preacher walked off into the deep dusk, fixin' to do his business. Which was when Dime started up a barking that sounded like the hounds of Hell, howling and snarling.

He listened for the sound of coyote or some such. Damned dog'd lost a leg to a pack of wild coyotes right near three years ago and was still mean as the dickens.

Still, Dime didn't let up and varmints didn't whisper 'shit,' clear as day, neither.

Fly still gaping wide open, Preacher turned in a circle, eyes searching the dark. "Whoever you are, stranger, we still got some biscuits and bacon, if you want to come on in and sit." He had always found it was better to offer than to have someone try to take.

"You make it a habit to invite strangers in?" That voice was gravelly and hoarse as a bullfrog's, plumb unreal. "What if I'm a Comanche?"

"Then the half-breed back there with the rifle will shoot you down. Come on, now. Out where I can see you." Preacher knew Bear had his back. The man might not speak, but he could hear better than Dime.

The night seemed to grow darker around the form of a tall man, hat hiding his face, holsters ready at his hips.

Preacher peered, taking in the stiff posture and the way the man walked on the balls of his feet, ready to go one way or the other. He waved back at Bear to stand down, and as if to break the tension, Abraham broke wind, loud and steady, making Dime whine.

"Howdy."

"Evenin'." The hat tipped back, just a touch, giving him a look at a jaw sharp as a spade. "Saw the fire and got to wonderin'. Ain't seen many folk out this way."

"No, sir, I imagine you hadn't. We're passing through on our way to Clark. You wantin' to sit a spell?"

"That'd be neighborly." The stranger came closer, staying well out of the firelight. "Y'all had other company tonight?"

"Nossir. We just came out of town this morning, been on our own ever since. You lookin' to cause trouble?"

"Nope." The stranger spit, shook his head. "Not a bit."

"Well, all right then." He felt a breeze and looked down, sighing again as he did up the buttons of his fly. "Come on and sit then. We've got coffee and food, like I said."

Very deliberately, Preacher turned his back on the man and headed back to the fire.

He was followed, the man's bootsteps quiet, steady behind him. Those jackrabbit long legs folded easy, sitting on a log set on the outside ring of the fire.

Bear came over with a plate of bacon, biscuits and beans. He'd moved the beans to a new pot, at least, and they tasted better for it. That Bear disapproved was obvious in his scowl, but one of the reasons Preacher kept him around was that he couldn't say a damned thing.

"Eat up."

"Mighty nice of you." That voice sent shivers up his spine like the sound of those souls taken to speaking in tongues. Course, that weren't nothing to the goosebumps he got when the light fell right, showing the scars on the stranger's throat, the kiss of a hanging rope.

"I might live to regret it. Mind if I smoke?" Well, that explained the voice right well, didn't it? Preacher wondered if the man deserved hanging or if he'd been in the wrong place at the right time.

"Nope." The beans were scarfed up like a hungry dog went at scraps, the stranger licking the ink-dark mustache clean and sopping the pot liquor up with the biscuit.

Preacher pulled out another cheroot, lighting up with a stick pulled out of the fire. He shifted as he did it, looking the stranger over right careful. Long and lean, dusty and worn, the man looked hard as boot leather. He sat still as the grave, the only spark of color in him eyes like chips of winter sky.

"There's more, you want some. Bear always has plenty of beans for Abraham." He waved at Abraham's sleeping form.

"I'm good. 'Preciate the offer." Abraham broke wind again, long and loud, and the stranger damn near smiled. "You got a musical friend there."

"He does love his beans. Probably cleaning out years of his own product. He sold snake oil. You got a name, stranger?" He was asking friendly like. He hated not having anything to call a man.

"Folks call me Hawk. Hawk Stanton."

"Nice to meet you. They call me Preacher." There. Now Mr. Hawk Stanton had something to call him, too. He smoked in silence for a bit, accepting the cup of coffee Bear brought him with a nod and a smile. He knew a peace offering when he saw one.

"Man of the cloth, are you? You find a lot of folks to spread the Good Word to?"

"Enough to keep me going from place to place. Some just come for the music and socializing." Some came to heckle, and some came to shoot up the place, but there were always a few of the faithful.

Hawk nodded. "There's always someone needin' to be told there's a good end coming."

"You know it." He drew hard on his cheroot before tossing it into the fire. "Where you headed?"

"West. South maybe. Depends."

Short answer for what was obviously a sensitive subject. He just nodded. "You on foot?"

"No." Hawk stood, whistled once, sharp and hard and the prettiest paint horse he'd seen came galloping up, head tossing, the rising dust making patterns in the firelight.

"Oh. Well, then. You're welcome to tie him up with ours, give him some feed. That's a nice bit of horseflesh." He didn't ask how a hanged man managed to hold onto a mount like that. Wasn't any of his business.

"He don't need tying, but I'll feed him, you don't mind. We've been running hard."

"Don't mind a bit." He knew all about running hard. "Bear will show you where the feed is."

"Thank you kindly." Hawk stood, nodded to Bear and him, the horse nudging one thin shoulder.

Preacher watched. You could tell a goodly bit about a man from the way he treated his horse, and this one was getting the full spoiled rotten treatment. Made a little of his worry fade, made him figure he wasn't gonna get his throat cut.

Hawk moved quietly, both horse and man keeping to the shadows. Lord, lord. There was a story there, yessir.

He'd either hear that story or the man would move on. Wasn't any sense fretting on it. Preacher took up his dipper of water and had a sip while Abraham provided a regular beat to drink by.

Hawk fed and cared for the horse, checking the beast's hooves and all.

When the feller came back, Preacher offered him some cold water. "You're welcome to spread your bedroll. I wouldn't get downwind of Abraham, but there's safety in numbers."

"I reckon that depends on who your numbers are, but one night won't hurt." Hawk took a swig, then rolled himself a smoke, offering Preacher some tobacco from the pouch.

"Thanks, but I've got a batch Bear rolled me. If I don't smoke 'em he puts sand in the beans. He's tetchy."

Hawk nodded, lit his smoke, icy eyes on the fire. "He don't talk much."

"He's only got half a tongue." Dime came limping up and Preacher scratched his ears. "This one's got enough voice for both of them."

"I hear that." Dime growled at Hawk and Hawk growled right back, doing a fair job at it, too.

Dime blinked, ears going up, and Preacher just laughed. Abraham snorted and sat right up, blinking at them, thin, red hair standing up everywhichways.

"Oh. I say. Who are you?"

Hawk looked over. "Just a stray. Hawk. Evenin'."

"Pleased to make your acquaintance, sir. I am Abraham Marjory. Lately of Kansas City." Abraham got up and hitched up his union suit. "If you will excuse me..."

Hawk nodded, scarred throat working, holding back laughter.

Abe scampered off and Preacher grinned over. "Well, at least once he comes back he'll stop making music."

That laugh finally broke free, rusty as an old gate. "Praise the Lord."

Chuckling, he offered another drink of water, nodding, settling in for the night. Wasn't near as tired as he had been. "That? Is a prayer I can get behind."

He surely could.

Maybe he could talk Mr. Hawk Stanton into riding on with them a few days. Preacher was thinking he wanted to hear that story more than he didn't want to, and the man was certainly intriguing. Dime snuggled up to his leg, Abraham moaned in the dark, and Preacher nodded to himself. He needed some new company. He'd work on the man. One thing he'd learned being a preacher.

And that was persuasion.

Chapter Two

The dream was the same, night after night. Unnatural coal black eyes staring him down, long bony fingers dropping a rough hank of rope around his neck. He could hear the damned horses, snorting and stamping, the scent of brimstone and fire strong and bitter in the back of his throat.

Hawk distantly remembered cussing up a storm, letting them no accounts that had hold of him know he weren't going nowhere easy. They might could take him to Hell, but he'd go fighting.

The bite of the rope in his throat weren't distant, though. It was a deep burn that broke him, bone-deep, left him to scream for a handful of heartbeats that lasted for a blasted eternity.

Hawk woke long before the sun did, gasping and choking a little on the scars, the dream, shuddering in his bedroll.

Shit and shinola, he'd surely like to sleep through to the dawn one time. Just one time. Or two.

Three'd be better.

He rolled out and headed away from the little light the banked fire gave to make water.

He heard Fred wandering up, hooves clip-clop familiar. The soft nose pushed roughly on his shoulder. "Yeah. Yeah. We'll go. I'm awake anyways, ain't I?"

"Well, that'd be a shame, you having to go on and leave. You have no idea what my Injun can do with breakfast." Shit a mile. That was the preacher, and he'd been so quiet out in the dark that he'd never even heard the feller.

He pushed his pecker into his kit, buttoned up. "Didn't reckon to wake you, Padre."

And he hadn't reckoned to steal nothing either.

A soft yet harsh laugh trailed over and a tiny light flared as the preacher struck a diablo, the smell of tobacco smoke coming strong all of a sudden. "You didn't wake me. Not by a long shot, son. Couldn't sleep, so I'm out here like a haint."

Hawk hid his shudder and nodded. "It's hell, when a man of the cloth can't rest his soul."

"Well, I suppose it's part of my penance. Want a smoke?" A small tobacco pouch resolved itself out of the dark. He could see Preacher's face in outline now, under the flat hat.

"Thank you kindly." He nodded, throat tightening a little in anticipation. It burned now, like it never had before.

"You're welcome." They said little while he rolled his smoke, and Preacher just handed over the burning butt of his own cheroot so

Hawk could light up. Once he'd blown out a stream of smoke, Preacher sighed. "Nights get long."

"Ain't that the truth." Truth be told, days could be long, too, that damned sun beating a man near to death.

"You should stay on with us a bit. We're moving on ourselves, I could use a man to ride with who still has a tongue and don't fart so much," Preacher said, surprising him a bit with the offer.

"You ain't worried about taking strangers in?" Either the man was loco or stupid.

"Depends on the stranger. You'll do." The cheroot sailed to the ground, making a tiny arc of light before Preacher stomped it out. Dawn was just starting to creep up on them, the sky going light in degrees.

Fred wandered over, snuffling and snorting at the man before nibbling at one sleeve. Well... Fred approved.

"Well, hello there. You're a fine one, you are." Looked like the preacher liked Fred all right, too. "You've a fine horse here, son."

"Or he's got me. We haven't come to terms with that quite yet."

This time the chuckle held not a hint of bitterness. "Well, now. That's how I feel about this crew I've got. Right down to the damned dog." Hawk looked back over his shoulder at the crew. Yeah, he reckoned. How a man came to be with an Injun, a foreigner and the ugliest dog on earth he didn't know.

He thought maybe he could stand to learn the story, though.

"They're... a right odd bunch, yessir."

"They are. So are you willing to make it one more?" He could see the gleam of the man's eyes now, too.

"I reckon y'all are eating better than I am. You'd best not expect me to pray." He didn't. Not anymore.

"No, sir. I don't ask that of anyone 'less they want to. I have my reasons for doing what I do, but I used to shun it myself." A sharp bark of laughter told him they were back to bitterness. "Hell, sometimes I think I made a mistake myself."

He didn't have a thing to say there, so he didn't. Shit, if the pretty little padre believed or not? Weren't even a bit of his problem.

"Well, shall we go on and see what Bear might start stirring up for breakfast? Since we're riding today he won't let Abraham eat beans."

That would be a help.

He spit into the ground, hiding his grin. "Well, praise the Lord."

Preacher clapped him on the back. "There, you see? We might just make a praying man out of you yet. You get Abraham and his donkey both a'passing gas on the trail and you start turning to God."

"Remind me to ride upwind."

"I'll do that, son." They rubbed shoulders a little as they headed back to camp, the soft clop of hooves following them. It felt odd, but not bad. Preacher had a bracing way about him. A sense of shared trouble.

Heaven knew he didn't have no lack of trouble. Might be nice to have some folks to share it with.

Sure enough, when they got back to camp, he smelled coffee, real coffee, not that damned chicory. It'd be nice to have some of that to share, too. The Injun grunted at them, hovering over the stirred up fire.

He tipped his hat, polite as he could be. He hadn't a bit of gripe against the Injuns. Not a bit.

"Ah, Bear, it smells good already. Have we any of those biscuits left from last night, or are you making new?" When the Indian waved a cast iron skillet, he figured that meant they would get fresh, and the preacher sort of made that right by nodding. "Ah, I see. Well, we have the makings."

The silver-haired man smiled at him. "We get a good many gifts of food. We have honey, even."

"I got some salt pork and some hard tack to pitch in." He had a wee stash of white sugar, too, and the tiniest little pouch of lemon candies, sour as an old woman and sweeter than a choirboy.

"Well, that sounds fine. And if you stay on with us you can help set up the tent. That's all I ask to share the food we get." He got a look from those eyes, hat tilting just so. "That and no borrowing trouble."

"I ain't never borrowed even a little of it." He earned it, full out. No question at all.

"Of course." The Indian grunted, the dog barked, and the damned Englishman farted. That, it seemed, was that.

Chapter Three

Three dust-filled, empty little towns later Hawk was still with them. The man's horse, Fred, was more talkative than he was, but Hawk pitched in and worked, and a man would hardly know he was there. Unless that man was aware of every move Hawk made, stealing glances out of the corners of his eyes.

Ridiculous to be so caught by someone who was entirely impossible, but there it was. Preacher looked at the horizon, taking his hat off to wipe his brow. They had provisioned the day before, for the good townspeople had told them they had three days of desert before the next small community, and so they were on their own.

Little Bear seemed completely pleased by this turn of events. So did Hawk, come to think on it. Abraham was the one who sat stiff and nervous on his donkey, searching the brush and rocks for animals or Indians.

"Would you calm down, Abraham?" he said. "We're unlikely to be overrun by giant lizards."

"So you say, sir, but I have seen no proof whatsoever that these lands are hospitable."

Hawk looked over, arched one pitch black eyebrow, but didn't say so much as a word.

Preacher hid a smile. Truly, it was almost as if he and Hawk shared a joke whenever Abraham initiated such a conversation. It eased his lonely soul. "Well, I did offer to let you shelter back in town."

"With those ruffians? I daresay they'd have me tied to the well to chase off wild dogs before you were out of sight."

Hawk spit and grinned. "Nah. Them dogs are good eatin'. You'da been bait."

A laugh welled in his chest and Preacher chuckled, the sounds hidden under Abraham's gasps and grunts. He winked at Hawk, feeling easier in his bones than he had in months.

It was the most fascinating thing - there were moments when Hawk seemed almost an old man, then other times where he seemed nearly young. The man never growled over being called 'son' or 'boy', but Preacher wondered if being called 'old man' would get any response either.

"Well, Bear? Where do you think we ought to hang our hats for the night?" They had maybe a good hour left of riding before they all got too damned tried and the dog's three legs gave out.

Bear grunted and pointed to the gathering darkness, then a bare escarpment a ways off. It would give them some shelter, some protection from the wind and the critters.

That would do them. He nodded. "Looks good, Bear." They turned just a bit south, heading that way, and Preacher nudged his mount over toward Hawk, lowering his voice. "You familiar with this land at all, son?"

"I am." A ghost of something passed over Hawk's face, something part sick and part scared and more than a little bit of fury. "I was born not a day's ride from here."

"Shall we move on before we camp, then?" He wanted to know what would put a look like that on Hawk's face, but he knew he had no right to ask.

Hawk looked up to the sky, squinted. "The clouds ain't black. I don't see no bad th... bad storms brewing. We'll manage a night."

"I meant in deference to your...upbringing here." That was quite a statement. Bad things...Yes, he knew all about that. Preacher looked at Dime, who ran back and forth between the horses and the sides of the trail, sniffing at this or that. No, no bad things.

"Ain't nobody here knows any Hawk. I can vouch for it."

The man would admit no weakness, he supposed. "Well, then, we'll make our camp." And be glad of it. His behind was hurtin' fierce.

"I'll ride ahead, see if I can't hunt up water." Hawk leaned some, that horse seeming to just know what the man was thinking and heading off.

Preacher sighed, watching the fine way the man sat a horse, letting himself stare a good long minute before turning his attention back to the trail. That man rode like he was born to it and, as he rode, it looked to Preacher like the light seemed to shun him and leave him in shadow.

Well, that was some trick of the clouds, wasn't it? "What's that?" he asked Abraham, who'd asked him something.

"I said do you think he will leave us out here to die?"

It took a full minute for Preacher to pick his jaw up off his chest. "Now, what on earth possessed you to think we can't survive without him? We got Bear. 'Sides, he's looking for water. That's what he said and I believe him."

Bear watched, grunted. Whether it was agreement of the fact the man was hunting water or that they'd survive just fine, he didn't know. Either way worked, he reckoned.

The shadows got long as they reached the escarpment, Bear moving straight away to get a fire on.

Preacher helped settle the horses as Abraham sacked out for a siesta, but once he got them fed and set he wandered, lighting up a cheroot. Bear hated it when Preacher left the safe confines of camp, but he didn't worry about what might be out there in the coming

dark. He worried more about what hid under
the faces of everyday people.

He heard a low, tuneless whistle coming
from the west. He couldn't tell how far away it
was, but he could hear it echoing, bouncing off
the stone. He hoped to god it was Hawk. If
they'd decided to camp out at some Robber's
Roost he would have to think about turning to
the other side.

As he got closer, he heard splashing and a
low laugh. "Back off, Fred. Can't a man warsh
the dust off his face?"

Well, that was indeed Hawk, and if there
was a spring or a watering hole the man was
holding out on him. Preacher snuck around an
outcropping of rock, looking.

Hawk had stripped his shirt off and was
filling skins with water. The long back was
tanned as an Indian's and twice as scarred up,
but it sure shined pretty in the fading sun, all
wet and slick.

For a bit all he heard was his own heavily
beating heart. He hadn't even let himself look
in so long. Hell, he hadn't even seen anyone
worth looking at in an age. This...well. Hawk
was worth the extra year he'd spend roasting in
Hell to have the thoughts he had now.

The dark hair looked damn near copper in
the last bit of sun. The black hat was sitting on
a rock a bit aways, along with the heavy
saddlebags. Fred was drinking deep, staying
close to Hawk like he was protecting the man.

Maybe he was. Hell, the horse was as tame as a dog. Tamer than Dime by a damned sight, long as he was with Hawk. Shifting from foot to foot, Preacher watched the shadows steal over Hawk, watched the way they dappled Hawk's skin, showing off the movement of the muscles beneath. His mouth was dry as a man who was recovering from a three day binge.

Hawk stood and stretched, waistband dark with water, hands reaching up toward the sky as he licked water off his mustache. "You gonna jus' watch or you gonna come wet your whistle?"

Shitfire. Preacher jumped a mile, but he figured he might as well not act like he'd done anything wrong, so he went on down the little grade and headed right to the water. "I din't want to bother you."

"It ain't no bother. Water's good and cool." That raspy voice would jar a rattler.

Preacher nodded slowly and doffed his hat, wondering at the wisdom of stripping to the waist with this man next to him. He'd never turned into a slavering beast before, though, no matter the temptation, so he shrugged off his long, black coat and undid the starched collar of his thin shirt. "It looks good."

"It feels like pure heaven." Those pale eyes dragged over him once, then skittered away like a new-penned horse.

His skin drew up like a cold breeze had started, and Preacher bent to cup water in his hands and pour it over his head. It also hid the evidence of his interest, which might well become inconvenient.

"I didn't think this place would still be here." Hawk squatted beside him, fingers dragging in the water.

Oh, that did indeed feel like heaven, even if it was slightly brackish on top. Once you got beneath you could tell it was a spring. He wet his face and chest, trying to ignore Hawk's heat.

"Where are we headed next?" Hawk's face was turned toward the south, almost looking for something.

"I'm figuring Inge. It's small, but that might be good for us..." The smaller towns seemed to breed the kinds of things Preacher lived to ferret out.

"You'd think more people would want to come and pray and tithe in the bigger cities."

"Oh, they come in droves. But that's not all that makes a successful tent meeting." He rocked back on his heels and looked at the sky himself, feeling the slightest breeze drying the water on his throat. God did provide, didn't he?

"What else is there?" He could hear Hawk breathing, the way the air rasped in and out of the mangled throat. The dark hair curled with sweat at the man's neck, just hiding the scars.

"There's special kinds of sinners." Preacher stood, letting water slide all the way to his waist. His pecker had gone right down at the thought of some of the things he'd seen. "Thank you for sharing the spring, son."

"You're welcome, Padre." Hawk stood, moving away from him and shrugging on the lawn shirt. "Some of us are special, that's for damn sure."

He sighed a little at the loss of all that fine skin, then turned back toward camp, pulling his own shirt over his wet body and grabbing his hat. "Now, I didn't mean you, son. You're not that kind."

"Preacher, you might know the Book, but you don't know me and, if I was still a believer, I'd pray you never knew my kind, neither."

Well, that was bald as anything, wasn't it?

He stopped Hawk with a hand on the man's shoulder, hoping he didn't offend or draw back a bunch of bloody nubs. "I'm pleased and proud to have met you, Hawk. Whatever you have been, you're a good man now. I'm a right good judge of character."

Hawk took a deep breath, head dipping a little. "I hope you're right, Padre. I surely do."

Squeezing, he nodded, moving just a bit closer. "I am. I know I am, Hawk. Trust me in this."

Hawk's nostrils flared, the barest shudder moving the man. "I'll do my best."

"I..." He hoped to Hell he wasn't making Hawk uncomfortable. Preacher took his hand back. "I'm sorry if I offended, son."

"It weren't me that was in danger of that, Padre. C'mon, Fred. Let's load up." Hawk turned and headed toward the saddlebags, a bulge in his kit that was unmistakable.

Well. If that didn't beat all. Smiling suddenly, Preacher followed Hawk, perhaps a bit too closely. "Surely there's no need to load Fred up again so close to camp. Let me carry those for you."

"They're awful heavy." Hawk dropped one arm down, hiding his hunger, or trying to.

"We'll walk slow." Oh, he was tempting fate, wasn't he? Pushing in beside Hawk he bumped hips, getting a good feel of Hawk's lean body, a good sense of the man's scent.

Rich and male and smelling of spring water and sweat - Hawk was enough to make a man fall into trouble.

He leaned a little, just soaking it up like he had the water and the sunlight, the feeling of touching another person so rare and wonderful that before he knew it his hand rested at Hawk's waist, his fingers massaging a bit.

"Padre, you're hunting trouble..." Hawk's breath sped, the scent of desire stronger, undeniable.

"I imagine I am, but it feels like I'm doing right, just at this moment." His own breathing went all uneven and rough, and he touched a little higher on Hawk's back, tracing the scars, thinking how that skin had looked in the sun. "I...damn, Hawk. Damn."

Hawk stopped walking, a raw groan filling the air. "Yeah, Preacher."

Well, that sounded like an invitation if he'd ever heard one, and he'd had more than a few back when his hair'd been more gold than silver. Preacher turned just so, letting his mouth trail across Hawk's jaw. Just like that.

The stubble there was rough and wiry, tickling his lips and dragging against them. Lord, the man tasted just fine, just like he smelled. A little dusty, a little sweaty, but all man, and Preacher needed that with a sudden, shocking passion. He swung them about, meeting Hawk's mouth full on, knowing it might surprise Hawk into running, but wanting it all the same.

The sound that tore from Hawk vibrated down into him, the saddlebags landing on the ground with a crash as long hands wrapped around his arms and tugged him closer.

Lord love him. Preacher wrapped his arms around Hawk's back, pulling him up so they touched all along their bodies. So Hawk's prick pressed against him through their clothes.

Hawk walked him back a few steps, his back coming smack against the rock. Those lean hips moved as if they had a mind of their own and all the while their tongues flicked and moved, the motions desperate and furtive.

Feeling the wildness, Preacher shook his hat off, his hands shoving at Hawk's shirt, wanting that fine skin. Oh. Hot. Good. His own hips rocked up and up, trying to get more.

Thank the Lord Hawk hadn't taken time to do up the buttons. He let his fingers slide against heated skin, the muscles there rippling and jerking with their motions. Preacher touched like a blind man learning someone, his fingers sliding over every plane and scar and nook and cranny, counting ribs. This might be his only chance. He had to make it count.

The sounds that poured out of Hawk did naught but enflame him, encourage one touch to turn to two, then three. The way that firm, tanned body rubbed against him did the job as well, making him figure he might not be utterly insane, or at least not alone in the insanity.

When they had to part to breathe, Preacher let his mouth wander back down over that bristly chin that was so much rougher than that soft mustache, down to Hawk's throat. The scars there were ropy and thick, one ridge after another, fascinating his tongue as he traced each line.

Hawk seemed to stop breathing as he moved, his lips and tongue lingering, his own moans shockingly loud in his own ears. There was something about Hawk's scars, something important, and Preacher gave them all of the respect they deserved.

The lean chest hitched, almost as if in a sob, long fingers tangled up in his hair, trembling like a leaf in the wind.

Preacher leaned back to meet those ice chip eyes with his own, staring at Hawk, making sure...well. Making sure. "This is good, yeah? Real good."

Hawk stared at him, nostrils flaring. "Yes..."

The word was almost hissed, but then Hawk took his mouth and he found he no longer cared.

Leaning into that kiss as if it was water and he was a parched man, Preacher let Hawk taste him, opening right up and moaning, his hands on Hawk's head. He held the man to him and kissed and licked and touched, his hips moving faster and faster.

One of Hawk's hands landed on his hip, moving him just so and oh. Oh. They fit there, hand-in-glove, both grunting into a kiss that was suddenly fierce.

Teeth clashed against lips, and Preacher tasted blood as he humped like Dime on a bitch in heat. He just couldn't stop himself, roaring toward completion in too much of a hurry, the heat between them making him dizzy.

The hand at his rear squeezed and tugged and Hawk bucked, going stiff against him, a sharp cry bit off before it could escape.

"Uhnn." The sound left him before he could stop it, his little death stealing the rest of his breath as his seed left him, right there with his pants still on. He couldn't remember the last time that happened.

They stood together, hearts pounding furiously, the scent of men and salt on the air. Hawk didn't say a word, but didn't pull away, just stood there as the sun set.

Preacher leaned in, his movement slow and delicate as anything, and put a kiss to the corner of Hawk's mouth. Then he shook his head. "Good thing we're still at the spring." The silence cracked like ice on a pond.

Hawk nodded, swallowed hard enough that he heard it. "You can take the skins with you after you're cleaned up; they'll come looking. I'll come along shortly."

"Are you..." Preacher cleared his throat, cutting off all of his questions. "I'll do that." His hand traced Hawk's cheek, his fingers lingering before he turned away and walked back to the spring.

Hawk's shadow fell across him as the man knelt to wet a cloth. "I ain't gonna mar your name with your men."

"You couldn't, not for this. Bear ain't got no care for what I do, and Abraham doesn't know his prick is worth more than pissing. And I'm my own man, Hawk. I'd do it again." And again and again if Hawk let him.

One hand reached out, finger tracing his shoulder. "It's worth doing again."

"It is, Hawk. It surely is." They stared at each other again for a good long while before he smiled wryly. "Well, we'd best get on."

"Yessir. It's too close to pure dark to be wandering out here."

"Yeah. Things come on out in the dark." Quickly, Preacher undid his pants and washed up before buttoning back up and grabbing the water skins. "You come on right behind me. Not losing you now, for sure."

"Fred makes sure I keep to the right path. I'll be there, sure as dawn."

"I'll look forward to seeing you there, Hawk. I surely will." Somehow he couldn't bring himself to call Hawk 'son' anymore.

Hell, somehow that suited him just fine.

***

They ate well, frying some bacon to add to the beans, some flapjacks with dried apple on the side. Hawk saved one leathery piece of apple out, chewing on it, letting the sweetness fill him up.

He'd traded for some sorghum candy in town, too. It would get him through more than a week without craving.

He pulled out his knife and his whetstone, eyes drawn over to the shadowed face, the cherry-red light of the cheroot. He could just sit and stare, given a chance. Silver-haired, but not old, no sir. That jaw was strong and the laugh lines beside the muddy-water eyes just fascinated him.

Preacher.

Hawk swallowed, the sweet of the apple easing the way. What they'd done at the spring seemed distant, somehow. Another dream in a series of phantasms that went on and on.

Preacher seemed to have forgotten it for sure, chatting easily with the Englishman and patting the dog as he smoked. Every so often those dark eyes, nearly black he'd found up close, would cut over to him, and Preacher would smile a bit. Just like he had the night before, nothing else there but pleasantry.

Maybe.

Maybe it had been a vision - too much sun and too little water and sleep. Maybe this place was just haunting him.

Maybe...

Hawk's throat tightened and he stood, heading away from the firelight, into the shadows so he could catch his breath. Fred was right there, nose at his shoulder, watching him.

It wasn't long before the red glow of a cheroot lit up the space a few feet away, Preacher coming on out to catch up with him. "You all right, Hawk? Anything I can do?"

"I..." He coughed a little, trying to clear his throat. "I'm good, Padre. Needed to stretch my legs."

The cheroot flew to the ground and Preacher stomped it, leaving it darker. So it surprised the Hell out of him when Preacher's fingers landed on his collar, just sliding above to touch his throat. "Does it give you trouble?"

He caught himself nodding before he even thought about it. It burned him, the raw ache constant and sure as the dawn, reminding him of the rope, the black laughter all around him as it jerked.

"You sounded raw." Warm and firm, those fingers traced his skin, so gentle, seeming to ease the ache.

"Never gonna be a songbird." His chin lifted, eyes searching the black sky with its pinpoints of light.

"No, sir. It suits you, though. Which I suppose ain't very Christian of me." That hand curled around the back of his neck, telling him before at the spring wasn't no dream, as it felt just the same.

He followed the gentle pressure, leaning toward Preacher, wanting to feel the brush and tickle of the pale mustache against his lips. "No one wants me singing praises anyway, Padre."

"No? I'll take your singing any day, Hawk." He noticed the "son" was long gone, and that too, told him he wasn't imagining. Preacher gave him what he wanted, a kiss brushing his mouth, their mustaches tickling together.

Smoke. Preacher tasted like hunger and smoke and Hawk reckoned a man could learn to need that on his tongue. Preacher touched him with the other hand, too, cupping the back of his head, holding him there. The man liked to pet, touch, and feel. It could make him crazy.

He reached out, hands landing on Preacher's hips. His thumbs drew circles on the pointed hipbones, a dull ball of fire burning in his gut.

"Makin' me ache." Preacher nibbled across to lick under his ear, seeking out all of his sensitive spots. The man's hips rocked against him, pushing into his hands.

His breath caught again like it was rainwater and his own wantin' a dam.

The man's mouth moved, too, sliding on his skin, drawn right back to his scars just like before. Preacher traced every one, and damned if the sting didn't ease a little, his raw throat relaxing.

Hawk took a deep, deep breath, this unnatural sound tearing from him as his prick jerked.

"Mmmhmm." Oh, that was purely not a sound a sky pilot should make. It was low and deep and full of all the need in the world.

"Yes..." The ground beneath his feet seemed to shift like quicksand, but it was just him. Just him and the padre.

They...well, they sank to their knees on the ground, their mouths moving together, hands pulling at clothes. It felt like Hellfire, as hot as they were. Felt like Heaven, too.

His mouth dragged over each bit of tanned skin he tugged the cloth off of, licking and tasting salt and sweat and smoke.

"Oh. Oh, oh, oh." Looked like the preacher man liked to make noise. Hawk figured he'd have to kiss him quiet. Those hands made him want to moan, too, as they pushed the shirt off his back.

"Mmmhmm." His teeth tested the give of Preacher's skin, his lips fastening right quick on the join of neck and shoulder.

That lean body arched against him, pushing and pushing, Preacher's hands getting greedy and dipping below the waist of his pants. The tips of Preacher's fingers just touched the top of his ass, so hot they liked to burn.

His ass cheeks went tight as a three-dollar mule's, just that one touch enough to drive pure need through him.

"Hawk..." The deep sound almost covered the noise of his top button popping off, and his pants let loose, sliding down off his hips. Preacher rubbed him, loving on him like mad.

"Please." His Johnson slid on Preacher's bare belly. The very tip caught on the soft skin, making him cry out, head slamming back.

"Yes. I. Yes." Preacher reached right down and grabbed him, hand closing on his prick tight and good, pumping up and down. Lord. That was. Damn.

A better man would get his head together, reach for the hard flesh waiting, but he couldn't reckon it, couldn't see past the white-lightning feelings filling him.

If Preacher minded it didn't show. The man stared at him through the dark, those eyes shining, that hand never letting up on him one bit. When words started falling willy nilly from Preacher's lips, Hawk kissed him, shutting them off.

His own sounds came free like a mustang when it saw the fence broke, pushing right into Preacher's lips. Lord love him the man just kept touching, kept kissing, one rough thumb pushing up along the underside of his prick, rubbing hard. Making his toes curl right up.

He was. It. Oh. Oh. He. His entire body bucked, seed pouring from him like liquid flame.

Gasping, Preacher rocked against him, the sounds and scents telling him how he'd affected the man, how Preacher was right behind him without even the touch of his hand.

He took the man's mouth like he meant it, swallowing the cries as the padre found his satisfaction and gave it up.

They finally slumped together, Preacher's hand still cradling him, their faces resting in the crooks of each others' necks. The sweat started to dry in the evening air as they panted, making goosebumps rise up. It was easy as pie to lick and kiss the skin under his mouth, to thank the man for this... thing they found.

Now Preacher was silent again, nodding against his neck like he'd said something, hands on the small of his back. They sat that way a few more minutes before Preacher pulled away, clearly reluctant.

"Wind's picking up." His fingers itched to reach out, touch the pale line of hair on Preacher's lower belly that just caught the moonlight.

"It is. Smells almost like rain, too. But it's clean. Not. Not..." Shrugging, Preacher leaned in again and kissed the corner of his mouth. "We oughta go back to camp, but I surely don't want to."

"I hear that." He found a kerchief in his clothes, offered it over. "Gonna smell us all night."

"Yes, indeed." Not that Preacher sounded put out. Not one bit. In fact he thought that might be bone deep satisfaction in those words.

The pup started barking some, the sound making him jump a little as it echoed against the stone. Must be a snake or something.

Preacher put himself away before handing the kerchief back. "Best see what that's about."

"Snakes." Must be. There weren't no storms brewing.

"You never know, Hawk." That look. Well, it told him Preacher knew more than most about things that lurked in the dark, just like he did. "I like to be safe."

Things weren't safe around him. Never had been. Was a damned shame, too.

"You coming?" Like Preacher had heard him thinking, the man grinned, teeth flashing white in the night. "I'd feel better with you at my back."

"I'm right with you." Trouble might follow him, but he'd kick trouble's ass on a dare.

They headed back to camp, the dog's barking going from normal to ecstatic, making Preacher pick 'em up and put 'em down in front of him. "What the Hell's got into you, Dime?" Preacher asked, breaking into the firelight.

Hawk sniffed, looking around. Things looked okay. "Maybe he just don't like you wandering in the dark."

"Maybe."

That floppy-eared, red dog came right up to him and nudged his leg, so it wasn't him the darned thing was protesting. Then the mutt went on to Preacher, wagging like mad, butt moving as hard as its tail.

Had to appreciate a man that a dog loved.

"Coffee," Abraham blurted, holding out a cup to him.

"Thank you, sir." He nodded and almost smiled. He figured if he showed his teeth, the Englishman might fall down dead.

"I. Yes. Quite." Poor red-headed feller had a nervous disposition.

The coffee was damn bitter and good and he walked a bit, circling the firelight, looking out into the shadows.

Just to make sure.

Nothing ruffled his feathers, no unnatural breeze or thunder. Just the night, thick as cream on cobbler. Preacher finally joined him, the hound dog following, snuffling along, tail as straight as a stick. "I suppose he was just excited by a snake, like you said."

"Sure. What else could it be?" There weren't nothing in the dark.

Nothing.

"Well, I sure am glad it's just...a dog's fancy. Smoke?" Preacher offered him a rolled cheroot and took his coffee, sipping right where he'd put his mouth.

"Thank you." He couldn't help but watch Preacher's mouth, admire the swollen redness of it.

"You're welcome." They shared a smile, Preacher's look warm and intimate, them eyes dark and sure and fine. Just like that.

He put the cheroot to his lips, took Preacher's wrist and lifted the burning smoke to light his own.

The pulse at Preacher's wrist went crazy, pounding for him. He thought sure he heard the man gasp, too, like they hadn't just had each other out in the dark.

He inhaled, fingers stroking over the web of veins, the surprisingly fine skin.

"Nothing as fine as a good smoke,"
Preacher said, the barest tremor in his voice.
"Is there? I tell you what."

"I can think of a few things." He reckoned
he could probably make himself a list.

That got him a look that seared him right to
his toes. "I bet. I." Preacher lowered his voice.
"We could move the bedrolls a little farther
from the fire. Abraham never strays more than
two feet from it and Bear sleeps like the dead."

"You swear that dog ain't jealous at night?"

"Pretty sure. I've never snuggled up to no
one else, though." That man had a laugh that
would shame the devil. Lord, lord.

"Well, if'n he goes for my balls, I expect
you to defend 'em." He couldn't help smiling
back, his own chuckle damn near unused.

"I promise. I'll defend them with my life,
Hawk." A man of his word, that Preacher.
Anyone could tell that.

"I'd take defending them like you would
your own. I won't need your life for them."
Hawk swallowed, took a deep drag on the
cheroot, the words echoing in his head.

"That's a promise, Hawk. It surely is."
Preacher nodded once, sharply, like that was
that. And maybe it was that damned easy.

"Then let's get some rest. Not every night's
quiet as this." In fact, some nights brought
storms.

Chapter Four

Town.

It was odd, because Preacher usually loved rolling into a new one, setting up his tent and offering to let all and sundry come to be cleansed. This time he was dreading it. They'd been out on the land for nearly three days, and while travel was arduous and dusty, the nights had been...a revelation.

He and Hawk had found each other in the dark, and if anyone objected they kept it to themselves. Not that anyone would save Dime, and he liked Hawk just fine. Hadn't bitten the man at all.

Inge was a good deal larger than Preacher had heard, having three different saloons and a hotel besides. Preacher had already talked to the local sky pilot and the town fathers, gotten permission to set up his tent the next day. Never did want to step on local toes. More than once that had ended with them on the run. Maybe they could have a night in town without too much trouble, not have to camp outside. He had a little stake put back.

"How do y'all feel about getting us some rooms? Bear, they say the Broken Lady saloon will take Injuns."

Hawk and Fred were both looking a little twitchy, a little like they didn't know what to think, all these folks around. Of course, people were staring, Hawk's icy eyes and scarred throat enough to scare a righteous man.

"We could always not," he said, hoping to put the man at ease.

"Oh, I should like a bath," Abraham said. "And a hot meal that has no beans in it."

Bear rolled his eyes a bit and Hawk snorted, grin wicked. "The whole town would be likin' that, now."

Dime barked, wagging like he agreed, too, making them all laugh.

"Well, whyn't we try to stay here in town tonight. We ain't got to go to the hotel. They tell me all of the saloons have beds without bugs, you got enough coin, and I have a bit put back."

"Do you need me to scope out a place for you to set up?" Hawk met his eyes and then growled at a group of women pointing and tittering behind their hands.

"Oh, I can come with you." He flipped a coin at Abraham. "You and Bear get us rooms. Find out how much a bath is. Hawk and I will scout until dark."

They headed out of town, both Hawk and Fred settling, calming right down. Lord have mercy, those two weren't social.

Preacher supposed it was just them being used to being on their own. "Better?" he asked, glancing over.

Hawk's chin dipped in a nod before the man cleared his throat. "I ain't much for crowded places."

"Well, then I suggest you stay away from the tent meeting tomorrow." He nudged his horse a little closer, so they were leg to leg. "It ought to be a good one."

"I will. I can't handle fire and brimstone no more."

He glanced over, wondering what that was about. Hell, maybe it was a group of zealots who had hung the man in the first place. Who knew? Hawk's secrets hung heavy between them sometimes. "Well, you can help us set up the tent and head out and smoke some. How about over there?"

Hawk looked over at the flat piece of land, the prairie grass waving and dappled with the sun. "It'll do. Hell, it's a nice, flat place."

"It is." The late afternoon light seemed almost too bright, too orange. Preacher looked the other direction. "Storm clouds boiling."

They were still far off, but coming on.

"Yeah. You'll have to sleep tight tonight, keep the rain out," Hawk said.

"I will? You're not...you're not coming in with me?"

Damn. Damn and damn.

"I didn't say that, though it'd be hard, to be close and let you be." Hawk's eyes were on the clouds.

"I was hopin' to get us a room, just you and me." A bed. A real bed. That would be something. That and a bath. Together.

"Oh." Those eyes landed on him, smile broke through like sun through the clouds. "That would be worth living through the storm."

An answering smile broke over his face, wide and happy. "Good. Well, good then. We'll do that. Storms bother you, I can tell."

"Yessir. There ain't nothing good travels with them there clouds." Hawk's fingers brushed over his scars, the ropy, white strings around his throat.

"I've seen some things..." He had. Some bad things. Some that tested his faith like nothing going. "Well, we found us a tent spot. Mark it for me, will you?" Preacher pulled a little, red flag on a stake out of his saddle bags.

"Sure enough." Hawk took it, rode over to set the stake. The wind started to blow some and Preacher swore he could hear something in the air - laughter, a low rumble. A hiss.

The hair rose on the back of his neck even as his gelding danced under him. "You hear that, Hawk?"

"Uh-huh." Hawk pulled his hat down low, hiding his face. "There's a bad one coming."

"We oughta get back to town, huh? Hole up in the room." He really felt the need to move, to run flat out and get a closed door between him and whatever was coming. It had that heaviness that came with something truly unholy, something he'd encountered a few times and didn't care to again if he could help it.

"Hell, yes." Hawk's voice was rougher than ever, and he'd never seen Fred toss and dance like that.

"Come on." Preacher spurred around toward town, his gelding running flat out, letting him know it wasn't just him, wasn't just the wind.

Fred nipped at their heels, Hawk spurring them faster until they barreled into town.

Most of the town seemed to feel the same way, because doors were locked up tight and windows were shut. He and Hawk stabled the horses, giving Fred a little sweet feed as a treat for leaving him behind. Then they hurried up the creaky back stairs to the saloon, Hawk waiting on the landing while Preacher went to find out what room they were in.

The folks in the saloon were riled, the air in the place charged, edgy. Preacher reckoned he could smell the fear. The feel in the air was just the kind to make men mutter, make their hair stand up, and if there was one thing that would make a hard man angry, it was being afraid of something he couldn't see.

The noise and stink was enough to rattle Preacher, make his stomach roll. Lord, he was glad he'd left Hawk in the back. These folks wouldn't have taken to him. He got up on the stairs, met Hawk with a strained smile. "Come on, let's get in."

"Yeah. Now. It's fixin' to come." Hawk's arm wrapped around his arm, held tight. "Where?"

"Up here." He dangled the heavy brass key and pointed, taking Hawk with him up the stairs. Their room was simple and not as clean as he would have liked, but the bed was the best thing, and the linens were fine. Just fine. Not a bug that he could see.

Hawk locked the door and pulled the shutters tight on the windows before lighting the lamp. The wind was howling, battering against the saloon, making the most unearthly noise a man could hear outside of a bad, bad place.

"Damn. That's some sound." Like hounds from Hell. Speaking of hounds, he'd not seen Dime. He hoped Abraham had snuck the silly mutt inside.

"Yeah. Better out than in." Hawk wandered, stared at him.

"Come sit with me." Preacher grinned, patting the bed, and feeling the awkwardness between them, being inside with the light.

Hawk took his hat off, then came to sit, those icy eyes watching him.

"I remember when I was first coming west as a child I thought a bed was a real luxury." He grinned. "Now I can feel that again. It'll seem decadent."

Hawk's fingers slid against the sheets, the sound raspy, scratchy. "I'm liking our door."

"It locks." That had to be the dumbest thing he'd said in a good bit, but Hawk didn't seem to mind. The man laughed at him, in fact.

"Keeps us in and them out." Hawk's hand scooted close to his.

"And keeps us from being...interrupted." He took Hawk's hand, the roughness of calluses so good and right, so real.

"I'd like that." Hawk winced as the rain started, but didn't look away from him.

"So would I." Leaning, ever so carefully, Preacher put his mouth against Hawk's, still watching the man's eyes.

It felt mighty different, doing this in the lamplight, not hurrying it at all. Felt good, though. Preacher opened up the kiss, his tongue touching Hawk's lower lip. It felt like lightning, that tiny touch, far larger than the storm outside. Hawk breathed right into his mouth, the soft, soft sound nearly thundering through him.

Cupping the back of Hawk's head more firmly, he tilted them both to get a better angle, pushing his tongue right inside Hawk's mouth. God that man tasted fine, hot and salty and addictive as laudanum. The kiss lasted longer than a drunkard's sermon, Hawk's tongue meeting his, sliding alongside.

Preacher pulled back to breathe, licking his own lips and feeling them tingle. He slid his thumb over Hawk's mouth. "All right?"

Hawk's chin dipped, hungry lips wrapping around his thumb and sucking. "Mmmhmm."

That little pull went right to his prick, making it throb behind the cloth of his pants. Preacher gasped, his hips rolling. "Better'n all right by a long shot."

There was a flash of pure heat in those blue eyes and a low sound vibrated around his thumb. That made him wonder what those lips would feel like, wrapped about some other bit of flesh.

That other bit of flesh leaped again and Preacher moaned, the sound almost shocking. "Hawk. I. Oh."

Hawk looked up, lips popping off his thumb. "I... You make me... I have a need."

"Whatever you want, Hawk. Anything." Somewhere an angel was falling from heaven, no doubt, but Preacher wanted so bad, needed so bad.

Hawk groaned, lips open as the man reached for him, hands wrapping around his hips. Those thumbs slid up and down his shaft, rubbing him. It felt like nothing else he'd ever had. Nothing. And that was with cloth still between them. Preacher's hips rose and fell even as his hands clenched behind Hawk's neck to pull the man in for another kiss. Then another and another.

"I need to see you in your altogether. Need to see it all." Hawk looked at him like a starving man looked upon a feast.

"I. Yes." Swallowing roughly, feeling like his throat was as dry as Hawk's always seemed to be, Preacher let go and stood, unbuttoning the stiff button at his collar.

Hawk sat back, watching him, staring into him. Each bit of skin that met the air was touched, caressed with callused fingers.

Preacher kept his eyes open with effort, watching Hawk watch him like the man's damned namesake. That was like a touch of its own, making his skin shiver and heat. The jacket and shirt fell to the floor before he started on the buttons of his fly.

As his cock pushed from his fly, Hawk moved, sliding between his legs and settling on the floor. His eyes went wide and he stared down, his right hand automatically reaching for Hawk's cheek, sliding down to brush the scarred throat. Hawk swallowed for him, let his fingers explore, soothe, stroke. The thunder crashed and Hawk groaned for him, leaned in close.

His prick strained out, finally touching Hawk's rough cheek, and Preacher cried out, his head falling back until all he could see was the stained ceiling.

Hot lips wrapped around the tip of his cock, Hawk's tongue slipping in to stroke the slit, collect the drops of liquid that gathered there.

"Oh. Oh, Goddamn." It came out like a prayer, hushed and full of awe. That was. He was. Oh, Holy Hell. Preacher thought he might just die.

His trousers were eased down, but he barely noticed as Hawk's head began to bob, mouth sliding further and further down on his flesh. Words started pouring out of him, curses and prayers, love words and then just sounds he couldn't even make out. Preacher lost all control, his hips pushing his prick in and out, his belly tight as a board as he thrust.

Hot hands slid beneath his rear, tugging him up, in, deeper. Hawk built a fire for him, the flames burning him alive.

The storm outside faded into nothingness. Nothing howled louder in his ears than his own heaving breath. He touched what he could, Hawk's face and neck and shoulders, but his hands felt clumsy.

The way Hawk pulled, the feel of Hawk's throat tight around him, the rush of breath sliding down his shaft - all these things liked to drive him to madness.

"I can't. Hawk, I swear. Gonna." He could feel his little death building up along his spine, ready to send him spinning.

Hawk's thumbs nudged his balls, the tug and ache curling his toes up right inside his boots.

That did it. He blew like the wind at the window, his prick jerking and shaking as he spent. Preacher groaned, clutching at Hawk, his whole body just feeling like it was coming apart.

That tongue lapped at him like he was sweet as cream, Hawk moaning as his prick got cleaned.

"I. Hawk." Sinking to his knees, Preacher cupped Hawk's cheek and kissed him hard, tasting himself there. It just...Lord. "What can I..."

"I... Please." Hawk twisted, rubbing against him like a bitch in heat, tongue pressing into his lips. "Please."

"Anything," he said again, echoing his words from before Hawk did... that. Then he dug in, undoing Hawk's buttons and pulling that thick prick right out into the air so he could stroke it and hold it.

Hawk's lips parted, that ringing cry winging out into the room and echoing. Hawk humped his hand, hips driving up toward his touch again and again. He remembered the touches that had enflamed him and worked them on Hawk. His thumb raked over the slit at the head, the soft skin of Hawk's foreskin moving back and forth a little under his grip. Their lips crashed together, Hawk's hunger strong enough to make his spent prick jerk, make his heart pick up a beat even as his hand sped.

So good. So urgent. Lightning crashed almost right outside their window, lighting up the whole room, making his hair stand up. Preacher jerked, his hand clamping down on Hawk's flesh, the pull hard and tight. Heat splashed over his fingers, Hawk's shout hidden in the clap of thunder that near shook the walls.

"Oh. Oh, yeah." He moaned, torn between kissing Hawk and licking his hand clean. He settled for both, just not in that order.

They pressed together, the kiss ringing through him. Hawk's hands cradled him, fingers sliding along his back.

Preacher chuckled. "That wasn't exactly in the bed, Hawk."

Hawk looked around, then the husky laughter began, filling up the empty places in the air. "We'll have to try again. Up there."

"We will. This time maybe I can hang on long enough to help you out, too. I swear, I haven't been that quick on the trigger since I was a lad." This man just made him forget everything. The thunder crashed again, and Preacher pulled Hawk up on the bed, needing to cover up against it.

Hawk pressed close, broadcloth rough against his skin. "I won't let it get at you."

"Let's get this off you." His hands scrabbled at Hawk's clothes. "This quilt looks clean enough and I want your skin on mine."

Oh, warm. Hawk's skin burned against him as the clothes were tossed away, both of them finally, blessedly bare as the day they were born.

They curled together under the quilt, Hawk blowing out the lamp before they got settled. His arms wrapped around Hawk's back and his chin rested on Hawk's shoulder. It was a fine place to be.

Not even the wind screaming at the shutters could change that.

Chapter Five

He could hear Preacher's voice, echoing out over the grass. Hawk stayed far enough away that he couldn't hear the words themselves, him and Fred wandering in the sun. The storms had passed in the night, the dark voices and sharp claws that followed the clouds gone.

He'd seen hints of them - a dead dog in the street, a broken window, claw marks along the rough wood building. But he had been safe with Preacher, hidden in the bed. Touching. Rubbing. Pushing together.

Fred tossed his head, jostling Hawk good and hard, nose pointing toward the hills, away from the tent. "Yeah, I reckon I feel it, too." There was something waiting on him. Something in the hills. Something that followed the storm.

Fred's ears swiveled back, the tiny crunch of a boot on rock his only warning that someone was coming up behind him. He breathed a little easier when it was just Little Bear, though, the Injun looking off into the distance, too.

"He ain't waitin' on you, Bear." Hawk wasn't sure how he knew that. How he knew

there was a man. How he knew that he didn't
want to go and see even a little.

Bear grunted, the sound guttural and harsh,
one hand making a symbol to ward off evil.
Dime, who had padded in behind Bear, barked
a little, hackles rising. Preacher's voice raised
some and Dime growled low, Fred dancing at
the sound. Well, damn. He swallowed around
the scars in his throat, the damned things
suddenly raw like they was brand new.

Bear near had him jumping out of his skin
when one big hand fell on his shoulder, the
other hand pointing off to the hills, a little to
the west of where he'd been looking. A curl of
smoke rose into the sky, black and oily.

Something like ice crawled up his spine,
making him jerk and stare. "Shit, marthy. You
reckon that's someone friendly?"

Bear shrugged, waving back toward the tent
meeting, where Preacher's voice rose to a
crescendo, and then the singing started. Oh, it
was almost over.

"I..." He looked back toward the smoke,
toward the danger that waited, then back
toward the danger that waited for him in
Preacher's tent. A man like him, he didn't have
no right going into a place of the Lord, where
people worshipped and meant it.

A little more urgent now, Bear took his
arm, pulling at him. Pulling him away from the
smoke signal, whatever it was. Back toward
Preacher.

"Okay. Okay, Bear. I hear what you're telling me." Hawk turned Fred away from the smoke, back toward the tent with the people pouring out of it.

Many of them looked at him and Bear askance as they got close, and he figured most of them might rather be in an Injun's company than his. Preacher, though. Well, that man's face purely lit up when he saw them.

"Hawk! Bear. I'm parched. What say we have a drink?"

"Did you sing your praises and pass the plate, Padre?" He slid down off Fred, growling a little at the looks people gave him.

"I certainly rained down Hellfire and brimstone. There's something about this town that just..." Preacher nodded and smiled at some bustled lady, but it didn't reach his eyes. "It gives me the itches."

He caught himself nodding, pulling his hat brim down. There was something here, sure enough, something that waited for them, or he was a hare-lipped goat. Just like that smoke, waiting in the distance.

Bear made an urgent motion with his hand, pointing back the way they'd come, and Preacher scanned the horizon, nodding. "I see. Any ideas what that smoke is, Hawk?"

"I. Someone caught in the storm, I reckon." Something waiting that the storm brought.

"Well, we'll keep an eye out," Preacher said, and Bear nodded sagely, like they knew and were waiting to take out the troublemaker...

"You want me to go take a look-see?" He wasn't a bit sure if he wanted Preacher to say yea or nay.

"No. Not without me." There was something in that smooth, preacher's voice. Something a little desperate. "Give me a half hour."

"I got all the time in the world." The urge to touch was damn near unbearable.

"I just got to talk to the town fathers. Usually I do three days worth of meetings, but I don't think...well. Be back in a minute." As Preacher passed him their hands touched, fingers brushing for a moment.

Something was going on that he didn't quite understand, something that everybody but him was in on. "Abraham? Y'all know what's out there?"

Abraham shifted from foot to foot, looking uncomfortable as Hell. "I'm not sure this time," the little Englishman said, fingering his starched collar. "I've not been able to see as well since, well, since you came. Not that I mind! But Preacher is quite the, erm, well. He's good at dispatching evil things."

"See what?" His throat twinged and he rubbed at it, trying like all Hell to swallow.

"I. Goodness!" Farting explosively, Abraham ran off, clutching his hat to his head. "Pardon me!"

Hawk just sort of stood, stared at Dime. "That man's gonna blow one day and make a mighty mess."

Dime barked and whined. Bear laughed, the sound like a gourd rattle shaking. And finally Preacher came back, staring from one to the other of them. "I say we tear down and clear out."

"You get enough from passing the plate?" He itched to know what the Hell was going on out here.

"I did. We're good. Let's ride." Hell, Preacher looked ready to tear down the tent with his bare hands. He growled at Bear when the man didn't move fast enough, and he snarled at poor old Dime. "Where is Abraham?"

"His backside was fixin' to blow." He did his part, rolling the canvas and working alongside Bear.

"Damn that fool man. I told him to lay off the drink last night." Sighing, Preacher pulled up a stake, winding rope. "We just ain't ready to take this on."

"Take what on? What are y'all about?" He was getting damn tired of the runaround, now.

Preacher stopped, staring at him a minute. "I thought you knew. You kept going on about the storm. I just. Let's get packed up, and I'll tell you everything on the trail. Can you trust me that long?"

"I. Yeah. Yeah, Padre." He knew about the storms, knew that things followed them that hunted, that searched.

"Good." One hand covered his for a moment, squeezing. "Good. Thank you, Hawk. We just need to get out of this town. I think they're beyond redemption."

"No one's beyond that." The words surprised him, coming from nowhere he understood.

"No? Well, I'll take your word. But there's something out there waiting for us to leave and I don't think we have the manpower to fight it."

"So what? Y'all run from it?" He wasn't no coward, though if he could miss that black smoke he would.

"If we must. For now." Preacher stopped to rub the back of his neck, staring up at the sky. Damned if there wasn't a circle of buzzards starting out where that smoke was.

There wasn't a bit of anything good there; he felt it in his bones. "We oughta hustle."

"Yeah. Yeah, we ought." They moved faster, Abraham eventually joining them. The damned wind was picking up, another goddamned storm rolling in.

His skin crawled and he had to fight the urge to jump on Fred's back and run like the wind.

The last of the damned canvas finally fit into all of the bags and they were ready to go,

Dime dancing and barking, his little stump of a leg moving.

"We need to ride, Padre." Now. Right now.

"Let's go." Preacher swung into the saddle, heading out in the opposite direction of the storm. Bear gave a loud grunt and spurred on behind, leading the pack mules.

He gave Fred his head, the horse taking off like the hounds of Hell were set free and chasing them.

They ran until they couldn't, until they'd left Inge and everything in it far behind. The thunder and lightning became a distant memory.

But no matter how far away they got they could smell that smoke.

Chapter Six

Preacher sat at the fire, his head down, staring at his hands.

He knew it was the only thing to do, but he still had real reservations about just...up and leaving Inge to their fate. Because that's what he'd done. The whole tent meeting had gone from bad to worse, the mumbles and dark looks telling him his words about admitting sin and finding redemption were falling on deaf ears.

Worse than deaf. Uncaring.

There was a mark on that town. The mark of a people who had done evil and felt righteous about it.

The oncoming storm and the smoke of the distant roaring fire had told him... told him that something was coming for them, and that he didn't want to be there to see it.

He looked up, meeting Bear's gaze, those black Indian's eyes telling him he did the right thing. Abraham nodded, dozing, but every so often he would mumble a 'yes'. Dime slept. Hawk...

Well, Hawk still had a thousand questions burning in his eyes.

"Walk with me?" he asked, standing abruptly.

"Sure, Padre." Hawk's face had been hidden all night, that hat brim pulled low, but Hawk moved quick enough, boots kicking up sparks as he walked.

Preacher stuck his hands in his suspender straps and headed on into the dark, knowing what was out there was otherwise occupied. "What we left this morning... it wasn't something we could do anything about."

To his surprise, Hawk just nodded. "What's out there... it ain't no good. Pure black, but I don't see what that has to do with your tent meeting."

"The town. It was the town, Hawk. Not my tent meeting." The whole thing left an oily feeling in the pit of his belly, like meat gone bad.

"But..." Hawk looked over at him, something leaning toward guilt in those eyes. "I. How."

"I wish I knew what to tell you, Hawk. They. Well, I could see hatred in their eyes."

"So what? All them folks are just... lost? Seems odd."

"It does. But I couldn't seem to get through to them. And Abraham, well, he just couldn't even see the town." In a few years, the damned Englishman had said, it would be a salted hole.

"See the..." Hawk's eyes caught him, sharp and awake all of the sudden. "What does he see, Padre?"

"He sees things about what's coming, Hawk. Not all the time. He sure didn't see you coming..." And that had been momentous.

"No, no I don't reckon he would have." Hawk's fingers reached up, traced the rungs of scars around his throat.

"He can't see that town existing. At all." Lord. Preacher just gave right into the need to touch and reached out, stroking Hawk's neck.

"I don't see nothing but you and the firelight." Hawk leaned into his touch, throat working.

Moving closer, he let Hawk lean into him, let himself lean back. "They done something really wrong, Hawk. Something bad."

"He..." Hawk burned against him, almost like the man had a fever. "You reckon that's why the storm came?"

"I think so, yes. I think someone was going to pay. A lot of someones." He could feel it. Had been able to feel it, from boots to hat.

Hawk shuddered against him, just once, but hard enough to know it was real. "That's a big take, all them folks. A damned big feed."

"I know. I know it, and I. I would go back. I would, if I thought for one minute any of them, even *one*, wanted my help. But I can't...I can't save them all, Hawk."

"No. No, you can't. Can't nobody save them, so don't fret on it. You don't want to draw undue attention."

"No." Oh, thank the Lord. Hawk understood. Preacher let himself find Hawk's mouth with his, let himself sink into a kiss that surely made him a bad man. Hawk's fingers dug into his arms, pulling him up close and personal.

"Hawk." He said it softly, all hushed, like someone might hear, then kissed Hawk again and again.

Hawk wrapped close to him, almost like the rangy body was trying to protect him, shield him. Soft sounds pushed into his lips. Yes. He held Hawk closer still, pushing it, needing to feel, to know they were both alive and kicking. And not at the end of a rope.

They rubbed together like sticks trying to make a fire, Hawk's prick stiff as a poker against his hip. He put one hand on Hawk's ass and pulled, needing with all he had. He just. Yeah.

Hawk pushed into his britches, rough hand catching on his skin as more and more of them raw noises filled the air.

"Oh." His head fell back on his neck, his hips pushing up so his prick slid right into Hawk's hand. "Oh, that's good."

"You're good." The words were whispered against his jaw, closest thing he'd heard Hawk come to a prayer.

"Let me touch you, too." This was better than being in the hotel, which made him smile, because when they'd been in that bed he'd thought it was Heaven. But Hawk was a wild thing, something that shouldn't be walled in.

Teeth scraped against his skin as Hawk nodded, thumb rasping over the tip of his cock. Those lean hips twisted so that he could touch, could feel that stiff heat that waited on him.

This seemed familiar now, something they'd done more than once, but it still excited him beyond words. Preacher reached down and let his fingers slide between fabric and skin, touching Hawk with just his fingertips.

Hawk's prick jumped, pushed toward his hand as Hawk rippled against him. Those fingers around his own flesh squeezed like a vise for a moment, before settling back again.

It sent him right up on his tiptoes. "Hawk..." Lord, was that his voice?

"Yes." Hawk's eyes seemed to blaze in the darkness, the need and desire there enough to burn a man.

Hawk made him feel like he could climb mountains. He reached harder, got his hand around Hawk's prick and pulled, grunting as the pull on his own cock got stronger. Their mouths crashed together, Hawk's tongue pushing deep, parting his lips and tasting him. Preacher put his free arm around Hawk and held on, humping as he stroked. The kiss made his ears ring, bruised his lips until he knew it would show, but he just didn't care.

The wind picked up, carrying the scent of them - both of them - up to his nose. They were heady and strong, as rich as any male in rut. He wasn't gonna last long, not with Hawk there and alive and no storms around them, just that thick as molasses night. He stroked harder, needing Hawk with him.

The cries that pushed into his lips grew huskier, louder, Hawk's body licking against him like a flame.

He just couldn't hold it anymore, he just couldn't. It was too damned much for any man. Preacher came, seeing stars that sure weren't in the sky. His seed spilled right into Hawk's hand, just like that. Hawk stilled, hand holding his cock, everything gone slick and easy as Hawk's heat joined his own, drawn out by his hand.

"Oh. Lord, Lord. Yeah." That just. Damn. Yeah. Bless him, Hawk made everything that easy. That good.

Hawk's lips brushed his jaw, breath hot, steady. "So what next, Padre? We just ride on?"

"I don't know, Hawk. I don't know. I keep thinking there ought to be something...Salting the ground if nothing else."

"If you want, I'll stay back and do it. Me and Fred, we'll catch up."

"No!" Taking a deep breath, Preacher tamped down on the urge he had to scream. He wanted Hawk with him. "Besides, unless the sundry is still standing we'd have a time getting the salt we need."

Hawk nodded. "It ain't a tiny town, is it?" That was almost a grin.

"No, sir." He grinned himself, settling right down again. "If that's what we're going to do we need to ride on to Frio Nuevo and then come back. Or ask Bear, see if knows of some salt flats."

"I keep thinking, that smoke..." Hawk sighed, shook his head. "There ain't nothing good there. Not a thing. We gotta move away from it and not look back."

"Sure. Sure, all right." He'd trust in Hawk's instinct. "What do you think? Think we ought to avoid town for a few days? Put some miles on us?"

He felt it, the way Hawk went easy, that bow-string tension releasing with a sigh. "Yeah. Yeah, Padre. I reckon."

"Well, then, that's what we'll do. I'll have to talk to Abraham. Just to be on the safe side." That little Englishman could be shrewd as Hell.

"For all his stench, he's a good'un."

"Foreign and odd, but good." His hand still curled around Hawk's prick, and Preacher laughed a little, squeezing. "Lord, look at us."

"You do got some nice hands, Padre."
Hawk nuzzled his face, stubble scratching at
him.

"And your mouth is pure sin, Hawk. The
kind a man would go crazy for." He could see
himself getting to need it and need it.

"You're sane enough for me, now. I'll take
you as I get you."

"And I'll take you the same. Just...just stay
with me, Hawk." It felt like he was asking a
higher power, like he was begging.

"Until there ain't nothing left of me to hold
on, I swear."

That would be good enough for him,
Preacher thought, giving Hawk another kiss. It
surely would.

Chapter Seven

His skin itched him something fierce, way down deep where no scratching could settle it, and Hawk thought it might make him honest-to-Jehosephat crazy.

Preacher and them was having another of their tent meetings and seemed to him most all the town was there, which, he reckoned was the way it oughta be. Still, it made for a damn quiet town. Made him and Fred both twitchy as a long-tailed cat in a roomful of rockers.

He wandered along the dirt, the sun pounding on him as he looked for the sign that showed that folks could supply themselves. He was needing him some lemon candy, some tobacco, some...

A door popped open and a man stepped out, cast a shadow over his and stopped him still. Hawk's throat went hot and tight like someone'd found his hanging noose in his saddlebag and wrapped it back around.

The man tipped a wide brimmed, black hat that looked almost like Preacher's, but for the dip at the front. Nearly black eyes twinkled at him from beneath. "Good day to you, Brother."

"Not yours. Not anymore." His voice didn't sound like his, the words coming from him without his say-so.

"Oh, we're brothers under the skin, Hawk. Someday you'll come back to the fold." That voice sounded like a parody of Preacher, too. Bastard, trying to trick him.

Hawk growled, teeth baring even as the part of him that was *him* just blinked and spun, trying to figure which end was up.

"There, you see? Once you're in the Brotherhood, we never let you go." The man cracked his knuckles, loud as lightning, making Fred toss and dance. "Sadly, this town is as righteous as the last was corrupt. There's nothing for me here. I promise, however, that you will see me again."

"Next time you'll be the one swinging on the end of a rope. You should have finished the job."

Fred whinnied, rearing up, hooves flashing as he smacked the air.

"We should have." The feller backed right away from Fred, though, didn't he? "Next time."

Another tip of the hat and the man was gone, almost like he'd gone up in a cloud of smoke.

Hawk stood there in the center of town, teeth in his mouth, goosebumps raised up all over him like it had turned winter. Fred nudged him, got him walking again, until they were on the outskirts of town, staring out into the scrub brush.

Wasn't nothing out there 'cept maybe birds and coyotes. Not a thing. Not even a hint of anything. Damn it.

He looked over at Fred, thought for half a second about just running, moving so fast couldn't no one catch him.

Preacher was here, though, and he couldn't manage to leave the man.

He sat on his heels, watching the dust blow by until the tent meeting let out. Then he wandered on toward the tent like it was true north, drawn in spite of himself. Preacher was still in the tent, alone, sitting on one of the benches the town folk had let them use, his head bowed. The man wasn't all that old, for all that he had the gray hair, but his shoulders were bent now under the weight of leaving folks who might have needed his help.

Hawk didn't go in, just wandered at the entrance, watching, kinda drinking Preacher up.

When Preacher finally did look up it was with a smile. Preacher got up and came to him, putting a hand on his shoulder. "You're still here. Thank God."

"Yeah. You think I was fixin' to run?"

"I thought you might bolt. I hoped you wouldn't." That smile got wider and Preacher drew him into the tent for a quick, scorching kiss.

Hawk gathered Preacher to him, letting the man ease the ache and burn in his throat, deep in him.

They leaned on each other, Preacher seeming to take as much strength from him as he did from the padre. "It was better today."

"I know." He'd been told, hadn't he?

"You do? Were you listening? I thought sure you'd wandered too far..." He got a keen look, Preacher waiting, seeming to hardly breathe.

"I." Fred whinnied outside, making him jump. "I didn't get to supplying up."

"Well, that's all right. We can provision tomorrow. The Mayor's wife asked us all to supper. I refused, but she insisted on at least giving us a meal at the boarding house, so we'll eat good tonight."

"That's plumb neighborly, Padre. You sure you want me to sit in? I ain't spreading the word. I'm just riding along." Just riding along, leading the padre into temptation.

"Well, a lady like herself ain't coming to the boardinghouse, and I want you there, if you'll come." Lord, that smile would outshine the sun.

"I will." He found himself smiling right on back, his breath coming easier now, his aches faded.

"Good. They said they'd even let Bear eat in the kitchen, which is right down decent for uptight town folk." Preacher stroked his cheek, his throat. "You all right now?"

"I am." The padre always knew. Always. He didn't worry on it, just was thankful.

"Good. Good." Preacher leaned on him a little harder, seeming weary in his bones. "It's been a long day."

"Yes." His hands landed on Preacher's shoulders and started rubbing, eyes glancing out into the fading sunlight, watching the shadows on the outside of the tent.

"What's out there for you, Hawk? What makes you dream in the night?" That look was so damned knowing, too old for that face.

"Demons." His throat clenched, working hard as all get out. "My own demons."

"I promise, Hawk. I'll do whatever I can to help with those." Preacher kissed him again, slow and deep this time. "We should get on, tie up the tent."

"Get to your fancy, home-made vittles." They stood a second, grinning at each other like newborn fools.

"That as well. Come on, Hawk." They went out into the sun again, shoulder to shoulder, and damned if it didn't feel brighter, easier.

If he didn't feel like he might could face the nights that were coming.

Chapter Eight

Preacher looked at the shapes of houses in the distance, at the dust, at the folks as they headed back to their homes, filled with the fire. They were three towns away from Inge. They'd given some nasty storm clouds a wide berth. They'd almost lost Abraham's donkey to a rattlesnake, and in the middle of the night two nights ago they'd had a torrential downpour that had set the tent, which had gotten unwrapped a little in the wind, to mildewing.

He was starting to think they'd made a mistake, leaving like that. Leaving all those people... Oh, Hell, they deserved it, but he had a feeling something else, some other force, wanted him to go back and consecrate that ground.

Something powerful.

Preacher sighed, rubbing a hand over the back of his neck, staring at the tent where Bear had staked it out in the sun like a buffalo robe.

"Abraham. C'mere."

Abraham came over, holding his little bowler hat in his hands. "Yes? Do you need me to help with..." The Englishman trailed off when he saw his face. "Oh. Oh, I see."

"Do you? What do you see?"

Abraham frowned, turned half away, eyes searching for the horizon. That little hat all but crumpled under the force of Abraham's grip, and the red hair on the man's head waved in the sudden breeze. "There's a storm coming, my dear man. A terrible storm."

"What can we do?" His eyes automatically sought Hawk, needing to know the man was near. Amazing, how fast that dear form had become necessary. He'd counted once, how many times his eyes were drawn to Hawk in an hour's time. The answer had embarrassed the Hell out of him.

Hawk was brushing Fred, turned to pure shadow against the gold of the sun. The silhouette of that hat tilted, Hawk finding him across the way, meeting his gaze.

Preacher held those eyes as Abraham spoke. "It's behind us, but it will come for us, or we'll go to it. One way or the other it will be up to us to weather it and make it right."

Wasn't that always the answer? Weather things and make things right. Preacher'd rail against it, if it'd make the slightest difference.

"Well, I've never been no coward. We go back."

Abraham's eyes snapped back to his face. "Oh, do you think that's wise?"

"No. But it's what we'll do. You tell Bear, I'll go talk to Hawk." He hoped to God Hawk would come with him.

Abraham twirled that crushed hat around once, twice. "I. I believe Mr. Hawk is... haunted. Hunted."

"Ain't we all?" He wandered off like that was that, but he knew what Abraham meant. Hawk had a way. Preacher, though, he knew something even the seer didn't. Hawk was a damned good man now, whatever he'd been before. He knew it all the way down to his bones.

Hawk was right there, waiting on him and watching him with eyes like chips of sky. "Howdy, Padre. You look like a man with a calling."

"I suppose I am," he said, pulling out his tobacco pouch and grabbing a smoke. He lit up and handed the pouch to Hawk before he went on. "We gotta go back."

"No, you don't. There ain't nothing there for you." Hawk knew just where he was talking about, without him saying a word.

"No? The wind's calling my name, Hawk. Even Brother Abraham can hear it. And I ain't never been one to hide. At least not when I finally get my head around it." He just smiled, shaking his head a little.

"Well, then. I reckon I'm going with you, 'cause I don't like what's waiting on you." Hawk held his lips tight, but the man's eyes were sure and steady.

"I...thank you." The relief was crushing, surprising him by leaving him breathless. He was just gonna have to start believing Hawk wouldn't run.

Hawk leaned close - closer than was wise, probably - and stared into him. "I can't leave you to the vultures, Padre. There ain't a threat big enough for that. I ride with you."

He looked right back into those eyes, his body straining against the need for discretion. "I was hoping. I'd leave it all behind for you, God help me. But if I don't have to, I'm glad."

"You can't." There was a sudden flash of something in Hawk's eyes. "You can't do that. There's damnation for you there."

He touched, just a man's touch, a squeeze to one shoulder. "You know, don't you? You know what lies beyond that jumping off point. I can keep you from hitting that ever again."

"I. I." Hawk's eyes rolled like a mad bull's and he'd be damned if that horse of Hawk's didn't come storming up, hooves flashing and stamping into the dust, teeth bared as the critter screamed. Hawk jumped back, hands reaching up straightaway, fearless like the beast hadn't gone loco.

Preacher jumped back, hand reaching for a weapon he didn't wear anymore. Damn. Shitfire and damnation. "Hawk! God almighty look out."

"Can't hurt me." Hawk walked right into the flailing hooves, hands reaching for Fred's halter.

"What do you mean he can't? He's gone plumb crazy." That horse had fire in his eyes, for sure. Like he'd gone off eating bad oats.

Hawk grabbed that halter and tugged, and he'd be damned if Fred didn't settle, didn't stop and shake as Hawk muttered at him.

"You think he saw a rattler or sommat'?" he asked, watching his own hands shake. Lord, that was too damned close. Those hooves, Hawk's head...

"Something spooked him bad. He's good now." Hawk just held the big ole head, petting.

"Well, as long as he's all right now." That wasn't natural. No sir. There was something about the way that horse looked at him.

"He's good. He is. I'll walk him a bit, let him find his feet."

"I'll get us a room, then. Get washed up." He wanted. Well, he wanted things he ought to be grateful he got offered freely. He needed to stop wanting it more than anything else.

"Leave me a trail to find you." Hawk headed off, hat pulled down, a low whistle sounding.

That silly horse followed right along, nudging Hawk's shoulder like he was scolding. Preacher sighed, watching them go before heading off to order provisions. Then he'd find them a room and a bed and maybe a bath. Hawk would come back. He had the man's word.

***

Him and Fred rode and rode until Fred felt easy under him, until they were settled together.

The padre had scairt them both bad, jostling things inside his head that needed to be left to sleep, left silent and still. All he knew was that he couldn't let Preacher get damned for him.

He wouldn't.

Fred went easy into the stables, nosing him for carrots. He handed them over, stroked the soft nose. "I gotta get me some food, Fred. You hang tight. It's safe here."

Fred nickered at him and snorted, then he stepped out into the night, hunting the lamplight that meant food and friends and Preacher. Sure enough, there was a light on that called to him, right in the window of a two-story clapboard house. Must be that boardinghouse Preacher had told him about.

He knocked the dust off his heels, stomach growling loud as any dog as he headed up the crookedy steps and knocked.

A neat as a pin little lady with gray hair answered, smiling sweet as anything. "You must be Hawk, honey. Come in, come in. Your friends waited supper on you."

"Thank you, ma'am." He took his hat off, spinning it in his hands. "It smells fine in here." He wasn't so used to being in such neat digs.

"You can hang that right there." She pointed and waited for him to do just that before taking him into a dining room with curtains and tablecloths and the best smell he'd smelled in an age.

"Howdy." He sat in the empty spot beside the padre, nodding all around and feeling like things was all proper and all.

Preacher gave him a smile that lit up the night brighter than any lamp. "Hey there. Glad you made it."

"Me, too. Fred's settled in for the night. Y'all get the tent down?" Bowls started getting passed around - chicken and potatoes, gravy, greens. Heaven.

Pure Heaven.

"We did, indeed." Abraham just beamed, too. It was like good food made all the difference, because the little Englishman seemed brighter. Happier.

Of course, one bite of those greens and Hawk was willing to agree. Salty and bright and bitter and good - he shoveled them in, happy as all get out.

Preacher seemed focused on the biscuits. Light, fluffy, and served with plenty of real butter, they were a treat and a half. And watching the padre eat one... It was all Hawk could do not to stare. The man had this... tongue thing going on that made parts of him all tight and achy.

He got a sideways look, like Preacher *knew* darn his hide. But then they both got to eating and it just all tasted so good that he forgot the other for a bit.

Then the Missus brought out apple pie with slices of cheese on the top and Hawk reckoned he might just die happy.

"Oh, Missus Rockman, this is the finest meal I've had in I don't know how long. Thank you." He could see why people came to see the padre preach. He had a real way about him.

The lady blushed and fluttered, little hands moving like birds scared out of the brush. He hid his grin in the pie, not wanting to offend. For all her fluttering, she'd done a right nice job.

"You boys want some more pie?" she finally asked, and Abraham held out his plate so fast everyone laughed. Preacher, though, he shook his head, giving Hawk a look.

"I think I'll take myself off for a smoke, ma'am, but thank you, kindly."

Oh.

Oh, he didn't reckon the padre ought to have to smoke alone, no sir.

"I'm plumb full up, thankee. It was welcome though."

Preacher got up and ambled for the door, stopping to kiss the old lady's cheek. "Thank you again, ma'am." Then with one last long stare, Preacher stepped on out.

Hawk waited a bit, but excused himself as soon as he could, tipping his head to the lady.

"I'm gonna check my horse. Make sure he's settled in."

Then he headed out, eyes searching for his preacherman in the night.

The glow of Preacher's cheroot led him right on out where the night got too dark to tell where the sky ended and the ground began. "Smoke, Hawk?"

"I reckon I could." He took the pouch with a nod. "Supper was fine."

"It was, wasn't it? Good for the soul." Preacher's smile shone bright in the night for a moment. "Makes a man want to just snuggle up and get drowsy."

"It does." He kicked at a rock, watched it bounce into the dark. "You make a man want lots of things."

"Do I? You make me a little crazy, Hawk." Preacher moved close, smoke and man and dust on the breeze.

"I don't try to, but we sure manage it together somehow." His prick jerked, began to fill.

"We do. I'm not thinking blame, just the truth." Low, easy, Preacher's voice calmed even as it made him hard. "We've got a room."

"Just for two?" He wouldn't ask, but he could hope for it, sure enough.

"Yessir. Abraham said he'd rather not share and Bear and Dime will stay in the stable." The cheroot went flying and Preacher's hand landed on his shoulder.

He nearly moaned at that single touch, leaning right into it. "I could see a long night in a room."

"I could, too. I've got a powerful need." Fingers dug into the hard muscle across his shoulder. "I want everything you've got to give, Hawk."

He did moan then, deep and low, that touch echoing through him like nothing else.

"Yes." Just like that, Preacher moved in and kissed him, their hats falling to the ground as the brims hit hard. His lips bruised right up, hot and tingling under Preacher's mouth.

This was no easy thing they were finding. Hell, no. This was burning and aching and throbbing.

Preacher held to him, one arm slipping around his back to bend him to the kiss, making his boot heels dig into the ground. He could feel Preacher's hardness on him, against his hip, even through their clothes.

Their groans filled the air like the wind, just pouring from them both as they rubbed together in the dark. His fingers were wrapped around Preacher's hips, hauling them tight together. They rocked, Preacher rubbing up on him like it was the only thing on the man's mind. Like they had all night out here and didn't even need to be inside.

One of his hands managed to push between them, his fingers finding the curve of that heavy shaft, curling around it.

"Oh, Lord. Lord, have mercy. Hawk..." Preacher moved against him, panting, hands hard on his arms, his hips.

"Yeah. I got a need, Padre." Powerful need, sharp, just ringing through him. He rubbed and stroked, hips bucking and rolling like he was a dog.

It was like neither of them had a lick of sense, because they didn't move, they didn't hide, they just touched and stroked and humped. Preacher just knew now. Knew how to touch him.

He went up on his toes, muscles tight as boards. Heat poured through him like a wildfire, too big to hold it as seed sprayed from him.

Even though Preacher couldn't have felt it on his skin, the man groaned, face dropping to the curve of Hawk's neck and shoulder, and that covered cock jerked madly for him.

"We. There's a room. With a door." A place he could look his fill, explore the padre's skin in the dark.

"I say we go to it then." Preacher sounded dazed, like the whole idea was new to him, that room.

"Yeah. Yeah. I got... plans." They were wicked plans, too. Plans to last deep into the night.

"Let's go." Preacher took his hand and tugged him along like he was Fred on a bad day, eager as you please.

So he followed, just like he had been. He reckoned his place was set for now.

At least until he got cut loose to wander.

***

Their room seemed almost a copy of the last they'd shared, except for one little thing. There was no deadly storm outside to fear. When they locked the door behind them, Preacher took off his coat and shirt before going to the washbasin and pouring water on a cloth.

"Take those clothes off and I'll clean you up, then." He was a greedy bastard, but he wanted to see and touch that body.

Hawk's hat landed on the table, fingers working open his buttons. "You sure you want to get the dust off? I reckon it's the only thing holding me together."

"It's just an excuse to touch you," he said, his cheeks going hot. Lord, now he was saying it out loud.

"Well, then." Jacket and shirtsleeves came off and then those boots and britches, showing him all that long drink of water. Long and lean and scarred, Hawk was something else. The length of spine, the stretch of a muscled leg, well, damn. It made him glad to be alive. Hawk sat on the bed for him, not looking the least bit shy.

Preacher sighed, a long, happy sound, before wandering over and running the cloth over Hawk's throat. That was a sight a man could get to liking.

Hawk shuddered for him, that scarred flesh offered right up.

"That had to hurt," he said idly, feeling like a fool. He stroked the cloth over Hawk's cheeks, and the man didn't even blink. It was humbling, the implicit trust there.

"Burned like fire." Hawk's fingers trailed over his belly, sorta petting.

"Well, you came through strong, yeah?" The cloth scraped a little on the way back down, and Preacher went to rinse it, Hawk following along, making him laugh. He drew Hawk the few steps back to the bed, catching those smiling lips with his own. It was like their mustaches wanted to tie it up, the bristles pushing and sliding on each other. He bent to his work again eagerly, stroking the wet cloth over Hawk's chest, watching Hawk's nipples rise in response.

"Cheated the ones that strung me up, sure enough..." Hawk groaned, belly muscles rippling as the man's prick started to fill.

Fascinated, Preacher pushed the cloth down, cleaning seed off Hawk's belly. He watched that pretty cock as it flushed dark red, starting to throb in time with Hawk's heartbeat. The scent that rose had his mouth watering, and Preacher licked his lips to make sure he wasn't drooling like Dime.

"I. I ain't. Nobody's never done for me like you."

"I like doing it. I like it a lot." He pushed Hawk down and turned him about, cleaning his back, letting himself touch that hard muscled backside.

Hawk's moan was loud as all get out, long thighs parting just a little, just enough that he could touch the soft, soft skin of Hawk's inner thigh.

"You're a good looking man, Hawk You surely are." Scrubbing in circles, Preacher kept on washing, letting Hawk feel it on the tender insides of his legs.

Hawk spread for him, heavy sacs drawing up as the cloth brushed the sensitive skin.

"Yeah. Real good looking man. Lord." Preacher moved Hawk back around and bent, licking the tip of Hawk's prick, completely unable to resist.

"P...padre." Those icy eyes flew open, staring at him like he was manna in the desert.

"Mmmhmm." He rubbed his cheek there, feeling how soft Hawk's skin was, how hard underneath. Then he licked some more, letting his tongue rub around the tip.

Hawk swayed, fingers sliding through his hair. The flavor that filled his lips was salt and man and pure, delicious sin. Perfect. Damned perfect. Preacher sank deeper, his lips closing around Hawk's flesh so he could suck and suck, his eyes falling closed.

It took a few strokes, but Hawk began to move, taking his lips in long, steady strokes.

Moaning, he grabbed Hawk's hips and let the man have him, covering his lips with his teeth so he wouldn't hurt. The sounds that poured out of Hawk were purely obscene, almost growls as that heavy cock jerked and throbbed on his tongue. He needed more and Preacher took it, holding Hawk's hips in the air so he could pull on that prick, the musk and salt making him grunt and spank the air with his own hips.

He could feel Hawk's prick swell, a sharp cry echoing through the room as seed filled his lips, sprayed on his tongue.

Oh, a man could get used to that. Swallowing it all down, he licked his lips and pulled off, smiling up. "You liked that, huh?"

Hawk swayed and blinked down at him, a soft moan answer enough.

That demanded a kiss, and Preacher gave it, slipping up to sit next to Hawk on the bed and letting the man taste himself. He was fed one soft groan after another, Hawk's tongue exploring his mouth, sliding over his teeth.

Smiling into the kiss, he moved closer, rubbing up on the man, his prick aching. Yeah. That was the ticket. He needed so bad. Hawk spread for him, one leg sliding over his hip.

His cock nudged Hawk's soft ballsac, the heated skin a caress on its own.

"Oh, damn. Damn. Hawk." Lord, he was shaking like a man who teetered on the edge of being saved. He rubbed harder, his body so hot he thought he might just catch on fire.

"Too late to damn me, Padre. You're not careful, you might save me." Hawk grabbed his backside, pulled him hard.

"I'll try, lover. I surely will." He wanted Hawk with him, no doubt. For a good long time. "I need..."

"I'm yours." Hawk kissed him hard enough that the room spun, his breath caught in his chest.

"Yes. Oh, yes." His breath came short and his eyes clouded up and Preacher felt the pleasure rising up his spine. Soon. Soon.

Those eyes watched him, blue as a winter morning on the prairie. "Come on, now. I got you."

Groaning, Preacher let it go, let Hawk hold him and keep him safe as he humped and grunted, shooting harder than he could remember. And that was saying something of late.

That deep, raw voice murmured nonsense for him, the husky sound a hymn in and of itself. Hawk's cock was hard again, pushing at him, prodding, and Preacher wanted to feel Hawk's completion, too. Didn't want to be alone.

"Damn." He said it like a prayer, letting Hawk hold him, listening to Hawk's rough words and kissing that scarred throat. "Hawk. Now."

Hawk answered him, body and soul pouring out and splashing hot between them.

"Oh, Lord yes. Oh, Hawk." He'd always considered himself a man of few words unless he was preaching, but Hawk had him babbling, acting like the biggest fool in creation. Not that he was going to complain, no sir. He'd take what he was given and be grateful.

Hawk kept him close, fingers on his spine just petting like he was a fractious horse instead of a man gone purely boneless.

"Well, that was surely a good start." He smiled. A start. They had all night. Gracious. He'd be rode hard tomorrow...

"Mmmhmm. You'll be riding tender, if I do things right, I reckon," Hawk said, echoing his thoughts.

"You and me both, mister." He stroked Hawk's buttocks, just loving being able to touch at will. "You and me both. What say we get started, just in case something comes up?"

He got one of those rare laughs, Hawk's eyes smiling at him. "Oh. Something oughta, or we're doing something real wrong."

"There you go." He laughed right back, taking a kiss that curled his toes. He couldn't wait to get going again, so he just didn't.

Anything that good had to be a sin. But for Hawk? He'd repent later.

Much later.

Chapter Nine

"Honestly, Aquilon. You'd think you'd never been let loose from your tether before."

He heard something growl and rattle as the tall, thin man spoke, dark eyes staring down the length of a craggy nose that seemed sharp enough to slice the air.

Then he heard a voice too much like his snarl. "Carchion, I would slit you bladder to jaw, rather than hear your voice. Loose these damned chains before I break them."

Hawk frowned, tried to shake his head, feeling more than a touch addled when it didn't seem to listen to him, not one bit.

"If you could have, you would by now. You do my bidding and nothing more, Aquilon, or you will pay." The chains slid away, link by link, clanking loud.

Another low growl sounded and the dust and dry grass seemed to billow and move. "Your threats are more tiring than worrisome, my *lord*." That last word dripped with more venom than an angry rattler.

The long form seemed to tower over him, soaking in what little light there was. "I vow, Aquilon, you are more trouble to keep than you are valuable...maybe I should rid myself of you."

"Then who would gather your prey for you? Starvation suits you not at all."

A low growl was his only reply, that and a mighty shove that sent him sprawling. "Do your job, young one. Now. I hunger."

The dust felt rough and hot under his paws as he rolled and came up snapping, teeth clicking around his long tongue.

Hawk stopped and blinked. Paws.

Paws.

Then a fierce hunger stunned him and he howled, barreling toward the town, hidden between the hills.

He could hear the lord's voice ringing in his ears. "Bring me the sinners, Aquilon!"

Yes. Each and every one delivered at Carchion's cloven feet.

The dust puffed up, clogging his nostrils and causing him to choke and gag, his throat tight and burning with Hellfire.

Air.

Air.

Hawk thrashed, fighting for a breath, for his lungs to fill.

"Hawk! Hawk, you're gonna hurt yourself...or me." The last was barely a murmur, but he heard it.

His eyes flew open, the bedding tangled tight around him, breath whooshing from him. "Padre."

"I've got you." That voice came low and easy, soothing. "I got you. It was just a dream."

"Yeah. Yeah." A dream. A nightmare. A terror.

"Uh-huh. You okay, now?" Preacher kissed him, and that went a long way toward calming him, making him breathe easier. He nodded, hands trembling as they grasped at Preacher's arms, dragging them closer together. One of Preacher's arms wrapped around his back, holding him tight. Warm and firm, that body snugged right up against him, comforting him. "It's over."

"Yes. Yes. Finished." Whatever it was, whatever madness visited him, was done.

He got a kiss, Preacher opening his mouth and pushing in, hot and wet, tasting him deep. Made every other thought fly right out of his head. He arched beneath the kiss, his body beginning to respond, to relax and warm under the touches.

Smiling against his mouth, Preacher gave a short nod. "Mmmhmm. That's it, Hawk. Just us here. You and me."

And a bed beneath him.

"Yes. Just us." He reached around, the feel of bare skin fine under his hands, against his body.

Preacher moved against him, making the happiest, warmest noises, nothing like the rough cadence of his breath in his dreams.

"I reckon I'd've been better off dreaming of this."

"You should. Every night. I'll be right here." The man had an unnatural obsession with his throat, kissing and licking at it, following the ropes of scar. There was something about that touch, though, something that eased him deep down and let him take a full breath.

"There. That's it." Kissing his mouth, Preacher gave him time to settle before stroking a hand down his hip, wrist nudging his prick.

His Johnson perked and leapt at the touch, damn near begging for the padre's attention. He deepened the kiss, his moan muffled between their mouths.

Preacher was up, too, loving on him, prick hard on his belly. They moved together, rocking and kissing, just needing fierce all of a sudden. The room began to grow light as the sun rose, their motions more and more heated as their time behind locked door grew shorter.

Pushing his legs apart, Preacher settled down against him, lips on his chin and throat, licking and lapping. He kept hearing moans, hearing Preacher pant for breath. He left the dream and all his worries behind him, gulping in deep breaths, rolling beneath Preacher like they were riding, just like he was pushing Fred into a fine gallop, like being in a rocking chair.

Grunting, Preacher went right along with him, kissing him so hard his head got all swimmy. When those rough fingers touched his cock he thought his head might go right off. Pleasure and heat flooded him like he was caught in a spring rain and he cried out with it, his voice ringing out clear inside his own head.

"Yes. Yes, Hawk. Lord have mercy." The wet and hot of Preacher's come fell on his thigh, and Preacher's voice went all strangled as the man shot hard. "Yes."

His own seed rushed out of him in answer, warming his belly. The scent of them together was just fine.

Just fine, indeed.

"Mmmhmm. Good morning, Mister Hawk." Grinning, Preacher rubbed noses with him. "Better now?"

"Mmmhmm. Right as rain." He found a real, honest grin, settled to his bones. "Mornin', Padre."

"It is, innit it?" Preacher sighed, but didn't lose the smile, settling right in with him, arms good and tight around him. "We'll have to get up soon."

"Yessir, but we got a minute or two before we head out again." Before they faced their demons.

"We do. Time enough, I reckon. Think that widow lady will make us biscuits and bacon?" Preacher sounded wistful. That man did like his home-cooked food.

"She was casting eyes upon you, Padre. I reckon you might even get jam."

"Oh, I'd hate to mislead her. I got eyes only for one. Jam would be good, though." He got a wicked look, Preacher batting his eyelashes, which just made him laugh out loud.

"Look at you, being pure innocence. The things a man will do for sugar and berries on bread."

"Yessir. I do love that." Preacher kissed him again, licking at his mouth like *he* was the jam. "You taste just as good, though."

He was tickled at that. Right, salty 'ole him better'n sweets. Hell. "You can have both, right enough."

"Can I?" Preacher's cheeks heated. "Is it wrong to be thinking of eating jam off of you? That'd be like the best treat in the world."

"Only if'n you do it on the widow's dining table."

"No. No, that I wouldn't do. Can you see her face?" They laughed about that one, the bed shaking with it. Felt good just to relax and take pleasure in each other.

"Padre. There is some things no man wants to see when he's needin' and that widder's face is one of them."

Hooting, Preacher rolled against him, just laughing until tears came to his eyes. "You got that right, Hawk. It's like trying to eat when Abraham is a'fartin'."

"You don't tell no lie there. There's a powerful evil hiding in that man's backside, trying to sneak out."

"It is indeed. I think it's the price he pays for his gift." He had to look twice to see that Preacher was serious.

"That seems... kinda cruel." From what he saw, the man's gift weren't all that fine.

"We all pay a price. And you just haven't seen Abraham in real action. I think you scare him a bit." Little biting kisses stung along his chest in the wake of Preacher's mouth. It was like the man just couldn't stop touching him.

"I ain't scary, Padre." Much. Often. Anymore.

"No? You could be, I bet." Rolling to his back, Preacher stretched again before rising from the bed, giving him a Hell of a show. "It's nagging at me, Hawk. We need to go."

"Then let's hasta, Padre, and get the deed done." He wanted it over, behind them.

"Yeah. Yeah, we need to, damn it all. I can feel it." One big hand rubbed the back of Preacher's neck before the padre went to the basin to wash up, making him think of the bath he'd gotten the night before.

Good thing he'd woke up and got himself some, else his Johnson would wake up and try to pay attention again.

"The water's still clean enough, you want some." Preacher sniffed a shirt before putting it on, looking more like a padre every minute.

"'kay." He'd just get dusty again, but he reckoned he oughta shave his jaw off.

Preacher grinned. "Do I get to watch you shave?"

"You going to make certain I don't cut anything important?" It was easier to smile in the sunlight.

"I will. I'll even get you a hot towel, you want me to. I don't trust barbers much."

"No, I don't like having strange men at my throat with a razor neither." He'd let the padre near him with one, but that was the one man on a short list.

"Well, then, we'll help each other. You can trim me, too," Preacher said, stroking that mustache.

"You got yerself some of them little scissors in your pack? I got a blade and a strop."

"I do." Little, golden scissors appeared, fancy ones like a lady might use to cut hair. "My momma gave them to me when I was a lad," Preacher said when he saw Hawk staring.

"They're right pretty, Padre." The color of them caught his eyes, the light on the blades fascinating.

"Uh huh. I've hung onto them longer than just about anything 'cept Pappy's bible." Preacher handed them over and proceeded to try to whip up some soap.

He held them, the snip-snip sharp, seeming like they'd cut the air. "They're damn near like magic."

"Aren't they? I could give your hair a trim, too." Stepping up, Preacher spread his legs to stand between them, taking the brush to his face.

"If you would." His hands settled on his thighs, holding the pretty, little scissors tight.

"You bet." Preacher didn't say nothing about the scissors, just soaped him right up and gently shaved off the bristles on his chin. It surprised him, how good it felt, and he didn't hardly stiffen up when the padre moved down toward the scars on his throat.

The soap softened his hair right up, and sooner than he could blink two or three times Preacher was done and wiping him down with a wet towel. "You ready for that trim?"

"Surely. Am I a prize horse yet?"

"No, that would be Fred. Ain't never seen a horse like that one." One hand slid down his arm and Preacher touched his hand, waiting.

"There ain't another like him at all." He handed the scissors up, a memory of another pair held in tiny hands sudden and sure in his mind.

"Not a bit. He's one of a kind." Snip. Snip. Little hanks of hair fell all around, Preacher picking them up and tossing them into the rubbish bin.

"He is." That horse was too smart for his own good, really.

"There, now. You're looking right presentable. Guess I'm next." Bending, Preacher took a kiss before moving to sit on the bed and handing over the supplies.

He did his best with the soap and razor, didn't nick Preacher a bit. When he took up the scissors, though, he got another flash of a woman screaming, hands whacking off hanks of hair and throwing them in a fire, moaning a little girl's name over and over. Night terrors.

"You all right there, Hawk?" Those keen eyes didn't miss much, but Preacher didn't seem worried none, just lifted up so Hawk could get to his mustache.

"Just old thoughts, Padre. Hold still so's I don't make you all crookedy." He was right careful, trimming the ends just so. His Preacher did have himself a pretty mouth.

"Good deal. Thank you. I don't suppose you'd clean up my hair?" Preacher was wasting time, he could tell. Fighting the day.

"I can." He brushed his thumb against Preacher's mouth, stroking it a little, admiring.

The pad of his thumb got a wet, sucking kiss, Preacher's eyes twinkling.

"Now that'll make me right unsteady and you might end up looking half scalped."

"We couldn't have that. People don't trust a half-hairless sky pilot." They laughed together, both of them feeling the sun moving across the floor.

If it weren't for the fact that the dark followed behind that sun, Hawk reckoned it would be near perfect.

Chapter Ten

Preacher watched the grass blow in the breeze, his horse plodding along under him, head down and swaying. He feared he was making a hellacious mistake, but something was pulling at him, telling him he had to go back. Jett, the ornery old bastard, had told him to follow his instincts, always listen to them.

Jett had told him a lot in the time they rode together, before the man settled and got him a house in the woods, leaving Preacher to carry on.

"You ready to ride for redemption?" Jett had asked him many times in those first weeks. When he would nod, Jett would go on. "Well, it ain't easy. If it was, everyone would be saved and they wouldn't need us. So buck up."

That was just what he was doing, bucking up, listening to Jett's voice in his head telling him if he hadn't met Hawk he wouldn't have run in the first place and he wouldn't have to go back.

Glancing over, Preacher found Hawk watching him with those icy eyes, and Preacher smiled. It was worth it. Love was like redemption, wasn't it? If it was easy, no one would need the good Lord to help them through it.

They'd face whatever came together.

"Buck up, boy," he murmured under his breath. "We're ready to ride."

Chapter Eleven

They were almost back to Inge, the horizon showing them black, oily smoke. They'd all fallen silent as they came over the last rise, all but Dime, who was barking his damned fool head off.

Bear shifted, seeming uncomfortable as all get out, and Abraham farted, the sound loud and grating and not even a little funny.

Preacher pulled his horse up. "Bear, you might oughta stay here with the mules while we see what's what."

Bear turned those dark eyes on him, staring and still. It was enough to give a man shivers in the heat of the day.

He tilted his hat down over his eyes. "Yeah, well, I got to. Abraham?"

"If the Englishman wants to stay behind, he can, but me and Fred are riding with you." Hawk's voice was raw as if the man had gargled boiling oil.

"I knew you would."

"Well, I fear I will not. I am your friend, Preacher. But I believe it was my job to see you this far. If you come back out, I shall be waiting." Abraham turned his wee hat around and around, his red curls shining and wild.

Hawk's shadow crossed Abraham and the man shuddered, strong enough that he could see.

Well now. That was curious. Preacher nodded once, whistling for Dime, who barked and came on along as he started out. Hawk sure didn't let him get a bit ahead, riding right alongside with that wide-brimmed hat pulled down low.

"You ready for this, Hawk?" He'd asked that about fifty times on the ride out, and he knew the answer.

"I won't let you down, Padre. I'm right beside you." Sure as shit.

"You're solid as a rock. I sure do appreciate it..." he let out a low whistle, trying not to gag at the smell. "Would you look at that?"

Hawk groaned low, eyes trailing over the smoking lumps and bumps upon the road. The charred and broken remains of bones anchored down the bare remnants of cloth and hair.

A singed bonnet rolled along the dust, carried by the wind and Fred reared, stamping it into oblivion.

They just sat there for a minute after, before Preacher nudged his own snorting mount down into the valley, knowing he had to at least pray over these folks. He couldn't just leave them this way, even if he'd left them to it happening.

"What could do this, Hawk?"

"Why he could, once upon a time." The voice rolled over the air like an ague, making their teeth chatter. It came from a tall, pale man sitting upon a stone, picking his teeth with what seemed to be a lady's hat pin.

Preacher reached for a gun he didn't carry no more, his hand slapping air. His horse danced and neighed. "Who in Hell are you?" Preacher demanded.

The laugh he got in answer was vile, thick like burned meal in the pot. "I have gone by many names. Aquilon there knew me as Carchion, but I believe you can simply call me Master. It has such a lovely ring to it."

Hawk's hand was steady, pistol pointed dead center of the man's chest. "I will shoot you, mister."

The man clucked his tongue behind his teeth. "Now, now, dog. Master. Pay attention, please."

"I won't call you nothing but a dead man," Preacher said, the same old white hot rage that used to get him in big trouble filling him. "You ain't nothing to me."

"No? Perhaps not. I am something to your rather lessened compatriot, though." The man stood, grave dust seeming to fall from the dark clothes. "How very fall you've fallen, my faithful hunter. I told the others we should have watched you hang through to the end, that you were stronger than you seemed."

Preacher looked at Hawk, confused as Hell, then back at the man. "You did this to him? You hurt him? You sumbitch."

Without even a thought, Preacher sprang at the man, hands ready to claw his weird eyes right out.

He heard Hawk's cry, the sound all mingled up with a wicked laugh, then a blow took him. It caught his jaw and sent him tumbling, ass over teakettle, his whole world 'aspinning.

When the world came back from the grayed-out confusion, he could see Hawk dangling from the man's hands, body held up high in an impossibly strong grip.

"No!" His jaw felt right mangled, but he managed to get the cry to come out, crawling toward Hawk. "Fred! Help!"

The demon - because it had to be pure evil, Preacher thought he could feel the hatred pouring out, seeping into the dirt - was speaking, shaking Hawk like a dog shook a gopher. "Poor Aquilon. You have no memory of our hunts, do you? Of what you lost. Of the weak stupidity that cursed you. That gift I can give you, I believe you have truly earned it."

Preacher heard the creaking of those fingers as they squeezed around Hawk's throat and Fred made a sound that was unlike any scream he'd heard from a mount, the sunlight catching on the sharp hooves as they kicked.

Yes. Yes. If he could just get to his damned feet he'd fight, too. Lord help him, he prayed.

Lord help me. That blow had been like nothing he'd ever felt. He could see his fingers curl around that thing's ankle, could feel the awful cold. Hawk growled and, if he didn't know better, he would swear that the long fingers turned to claws, tearing into the demon's chest even as Fred's hooves tore into the back of it.

Things got hellacious fuzzy then, sights and sounds all confused, his fingers feeling like the one time he'd got frostbite.

He would swear later that he saw fur and fire, that blood rained down and that the screams were enough to make a dead man weep, but if it was true, the Lord kept it from him, kept the world distant and dark. It was Abraham's voice that brought him back to himself, the worried clucking and fretting as a cold cloth pressed against his face.

"Hawk?" He croaked it out, trying to turn his head and look, his skull aching.

"He went for more water. He suggested we wake you and ride north without waiting."

"No! No. Hawk..." He couldn't leave without Hawk. Hawk would run. Somehow he knew it. Not because he was a liar, but because of what...of what Preacher had seen. Hawk had promised to ride with him, but after this, he knew Hawk would think of himself as a danger.

"He said he'd follow close behind with the water. You were in no shape to ride alone."

"Neither was he." Damn it, they were treating him like an old fool. Preacher struggled to his knees. "Hawk!"

Dime barked and yapped, running from him to the hoof prints in the dust, leading toward the river.

Good old Dime. Pushing Abraham off, Preacher climbed to his feet, swaying. "Where's my horse? Now don't look at me like that, Bear. I appreciate what y'all are doing more than you know, but I have to find Hawk."

"Are you quite sure? He had a mad look in his eyes. As if… as if he might do harm."

"Yeah. Yeah, I'm sure. You need to find us a place to make camp. And don't take nothin' of this town with you, not even dust. You got it?"

He looked at Bear to make his point, because Abraham didn't have a careful bone in his body. Bear nodded, hand held out to steady him as he mounted. Bear understood. Bear knew.

He nodded to Bear seriously, and patted Abraham's hand when the man reached for him. "I'll be back, I promise."

He turned his horse toward the river, following Hawk's trail, his heart pounding as hard as his head. Preacher heard Hawk long before he saw the man, deep howls and anguished cries echoing against the stones, the water splashing violently. Sliding off his horse, he slipped up behind a rock, his bones creaking so loud anyone else might have heard him. Damnation.

Hawk was on his knees, shirt half-torn and hat flung away. There was a piece of rope in his hands, slamming into the riverbank again and again.

"Hawk." He gave up stealth and went sliding down the bank on his knees, his pants and shins ripping in concert. He put his arms around Hawk to stop that awful beating, like Hawk was some demented drummer. Hawk howled again, the sound more animal than man, filled with an agony he couldn't begin to understand.

Preacher just held on. That was all you could do when a man was drowning, sometimes. Just hold on.

The sounds finally, *finally* faded, the silence left behind almost as bad as the cries. They breathed together, slow and heavy like the air was thick.

His hands stroked Hawk's bare back, the sweat and dirt there mixing to form a gritty paste. He'd need to wash that off or it'd itch...

"I ain't no good man, Padre. I cain't be saved."

"Stop that right now. You're a good man, Hawk. Who knows that better than I do?" He wasn't gonna think about that thing they'd met, or what it had to say about what Hawk had been. No sir.

"I ain't." Hawk curled into himself, that damned rope biting into the callused hands. "I told that damned Englishman to take you north."

"Why? So you could leave me? You know Abraham doesn't have a bit of grit." Letting go with one hand, he stroked Hawk's cheek. "Whatever you was, you aren't now."

Hawk's eyes closed, shudders rocking the man. "There ain't no forgiving what I done. He was right. I weren't meant to live among men. I should've hanged."

Preacher didn't know whether to slap the man or shake him or kiss him stupid. "Then why are you? Why are you here with me? He coulda took you."

"I. I don't know. I don't know why he didn't." Hawk's eyes flew open like a broke shutter. "Did he hurt you?"

"Well, I ain't at my best." Now that Hawk was looking at him he knew he could win, could convince the man to stay.

"Next time I tell you we shouldn't oughta ride to a town, maybe you oughta listen, Padre."

"Rub it in, Mister. Just rub it in." Oh, God, what they'd survived. And only because that thing had wanted them to. Had wanted to hurt them. Jesus wept.

"You gotta ride, Preacher. We can't stay close. He wants..." Hawk sighed, shook his head some, dust turning that black hair damn near grey. "It don't matter, he can't have it, but we can't stay."

"No, there's no more we can do here." Rising, he pulled Hawk to his feet. He'd been wrong to come back, but a man doing wrong in the name of right, well, he could be forgiven, Preacher guessed. "I can't consecrate this ground." He'd been a fool to think he could.

"No. They gave it to him freely." Hawk stopped short, nostrils flaring. "He's on the move, Padre. There's storms on the air."

The sky had started to go dark sometime between the flopping next to Hawk and the talking, and Preacher stared, shivering in the wind. The clouds gathered like they was magic, doing from white to grey to black right before his eyes. A dull rage filled him; damn but he was tired of being pushed, being scairt. He weren't no coward. "Let it come, damn it."

"We need to... damn, Preacher! We need some shelter. I won't let him have at you." Hawk looked around, eyes rolling. "I was made close to here. I was hanged close to here."

"Come on, Hawk. Come on. We can find a place to hunker down. We can wait it out." He pulled at Hawk's shirt, at Hawk's shoulders, having no clue where to go.

"There's a cave. There's a cave I stayed in." Hawk's eyes scanned the skies, the rocks. "Fred! The cave! Our cave!"

Preacher blinked as that damned horse nodded and started moving, shoving Hawk hard between the shoulder blades.

Lord. Well, he'd put faith in that. Fred had never steered them wrong before. He grabbed onto Hawk and let the fucking horse move them, let himself stumble along. Dime followed along, growling and yipping in turns. That damn wind picked up, swirling around them like dust devils. Fred pushed them harder, the cave mouth coming visible as they followed a curve in the river.

Their boot heels slipped and slid, but they made it in, both of them flinching at the wind that howled past as they did. "Fred...Dime?"

"He can't touch Fred. He tried." Hawk whistled, bringing Dime clamoring into the cave to hide in the shadows.

"Oh. Well, all right." They sat, both of them breathing hard, and he could just see the gleam of Hawk's eyes.

The rain was close, was coming and Hawk moved back from the opening, drawing him along. The touch was surprisingly possessive, protective. It snapped something in him. Preacher lunged, surprising himself by taking Hawk down hard, his mouth crashing against Hawk's in a kiss that drew blood. He needed to feel. To be alive.

Hawk's hands grabbed at him, pulled him into the hard lines of Hawk's body. Yes. Yes. He'd been afraid Hawk would push him away, deny them both this – this thing that they'd figured out together.

He rolled them until he could straddle Hawk's body, pulling at the rough remains of Hawk's shirt. His hands found skin, the tight planes of muscle and the tiny points of Hawk's nipples.

Hawk arched into his touch, that skin like tanned leather, feverishly hot under his touch. "Preacher."

The rain started pounding the ground as the wind howled, screaming in something close to fury.

The wind could have its say. He was too wrapped up in Hawk to care. They kissed like they were starving, their teeth clacking together. He could feel it, when Hawk opened to him, trusted him to share this wildness between them.

They moved to their sides, hands rubbing, legs tangling. They could press and pull and kiss that way, could turn away from the wind.

Hawk worked his suspenders off, opened his pants and shoved them down. His prick liked that idea, jumping out to push against Hawk's bare belly. So hot, so damned needy, that's what he was, and he pushed at the thin fabric of Hawk's trousers, needing all of that skin, not just part of it.

It didn't take but a second for Hawk to pull away, stripping them both down to bare skin and spreading a bedroll for them. It weren't a fancy room with a ticked mattress and a locked door, but it was theirs.

They seemed to do better that way.

He cupped his hands behind Hawk's neck and pulled the man right to him, kissing deeper and harder, licking at Hawk's lower lip. Hawk groaned, shifting above him, their cocks sliding alongside one another, Hawk's thighs straddling his.

"Yeah. Yeah, Hawk. Harder." They'd leave burns on each other's skin at this rate, but it felt good, felt right.

Those blue eyes burned down at him as Hawk nodded, giving him everything he needed, everything he asked for.

His hand closed around their cocks, pulling at them, working them hard, harder than the storm outside. He could feel the burn all the way to his bones, Hawk like a furnace above him, making him ache and arch. Preacher gave in to it, biting hard just under Hawk's chin as he shot, his cock jerking in his hand. Against Hawk's and all over their skin.

Hawk's head fell back, giving him all of those scars to bite and lick before more seed spread between them, the scent of Hawk's mingling with his own.

"Oh. Oh, Hawk." All he could do was lie there and pant, listening to the storm as it moved right over their little cave.

"I got you. I won't never let him hurt you."

"And I will not let him ruin you, neither. You're a good man, Hawk. Never forget it." There. Let them all put that in their pipe and smoke it.

"I hope you're right, Padre. I surely do."

He didn't have to hope so. He knew it.

Now all they had to do was weather the storm.

Chapter Twelve

The storm passed with the dawn and they rode out.

He didn't say nothing about the things that he'd been shown and neither did Preacher. He didn't think on it. He didn't dream on it. He set his mind against it. The padre said he was a good man, believed he was. Hawk reckoned he could act like a good man.

Abraham stared at him some, and Bear didn't look at him at all for a long time, but Hawk just rode a bit aways, kept his hat pulled down low and his mouth shut and followed the rest of them as the padre hunted a new place to save souls.

Preacher seemed tired, but settled, snapping only once at Bear, who pushed him and pushed him with those silent looks that Hawk could see every time they stopped for water.

"Let's stop here for the night," Preacher said, pulling up at a small depression next to a muddy creek. "I don't think there's a town anywhere near."

"You mean you want to avoid having to speak." They all looked over at Abraham, Hawk swallowing down a growl as Preacher's cheeks heated with a dull shame.

"Well, I'm not feeling like I'd do a town any good, no." Preacher pushed his hat back, staring Abraham down.

Hawk watched, a rumbling little voice between his ears whispering that he was part of this discord, he was the cause of Preacher's worry. Fred stomped some, jostling him, shutting that voice right on up.

"Y'all want to sit and talk on it, we can do that after we make camp. I'm willing. But I won't apologize for wanting to lick my wounds a little before I go out and find new folks to preach to."

He didn't think Preacher needed to worry on it. The man seemed solid as a rock when he leveled a steady gaze at all of them, one by one.

Hawk didn't say one word 'bout it, one way or the other. Preacher could meet or not, it didn't make him no nevermind. "You want me to see if I can't rustle up some game?"

Nodding, Preacher gave him a smile, the lines around that fine mouth going deep. "You bet. Be nice to have something besides biscuits and beans."

"Yessir." He nodded and spurred Fred on, picking between the fallen rocks and the mesquite trees. He loaded up, watching for signs of javelina or doe or Hell, a nice fat bunny.

Once, Aquilon, you needed no assistance in the hunt.

His head near fell off his neck, he snapped it around so fast looking for that voice. He didn't see nothin', though, and Fred didn't so much as dance.

Shit. Okay, then. He weren't listening to this mess, was he? No, sir. Not at all. He weren't remembering shit left forgot. He weren't going back nowhere. He weren't hearing this.

What, Aquilon? You will pray to the suffering god for salvation? For silence? For peace?

"I cain't hear you. You just let me be, master!" His lips snapped shut, eyes rolling in his head. Mister. He'd meant mister.

Fred bucked and danced under him, jostling him enough that his mind got set back where it belonged. He whistled a little song he'd learned long ago, something about grace and being found, bending down low, ear to Fred's neck to settle them both.

The furious barking of a dog drowned out the voice this time, Dime running right up to him, tail wagging and stumpy leg running as hard as the other three. Looked like Dime was on his side, too.

"Hey there, pup. We ain't going to get much game with all of us chattering on like this." Still, he felt better with the silence gone.

The silly mutt bounced along beside him and damned if Dime didn't flush out some birds for him a ways down the trail. His aim was good and they fell, dead before they hit the ground and he'd be hornswoggled if he didn't have them two wild guinea hens, fat and sassy and fed on prairie grass.

Hell, Bear might even forgive him for whatever it was that pissed the Injun off most when he brought them in. Even Fred looked proud.

Hawk caught himself whistling for sure on the ride back, the happy sound fading once they got back into the open.

"What'd you bring us?" Preacher asked as he rode back into camp. "We heard the shots."

"Guineas. I got two." He held them up, grinning as Bear grunted and hurried over to take them right out of his hands.

"Well, then we'll eat good tonight." He got a smile that would light up the night when it came, and keep the voices away all night long, too.

A man could be forgiven if he puffed up some and he dug himself out a lemon candy and fed a strip of jerky to Dime, thanking the pup for his part in it. "Dime flushed 'em out, nice as you please."

"He's handy."

They both had to laugh because Dime danced, and Bear was making these happy noises, doing a little dance at the campfire, and the day before seemed a long way away.

He sat near to the fire, nodding at Preacher. "He's a good dog. Real good. Bone deep."

"He is. He's been with me ever since he lost his leg. I found him, nursed him up good." Those long dog ears got a good scratching from Preacher before Dime came right up to Hawk like he hardly ever had before.

Hawk reached out, petting as the critter wagged his whole backend. He opened his little packet of lemon candies, offered one to Preacher.

"Thank you." Rough fingers covered his, stroking the back of his hand. "They're good."

He dared to let his fingers squeeze the padre's, just a little bit. "They are."

"Where do you think we ought to head next?"

Hawk chewed his lip and thought on that. "There ain't much but Injuns due north and Mexico due south."

Preacher sighed. "Well, then, we need to circle back around, huh?" The man just looked slumped and unhappy, too.

"Or we can pitch a tent and rest a bit." It didn't matter none to him. Not at all.

"That sounds like a fine plan. Figure out...figure where to go from here." He could see where Preacher's mind was going, heat coming up in those eyes.

He nodded. "Let ourselves... settle our brains."

"Yes. Among other things."

Bear snorted loud, making them grin like a pair of fools. His cheeks pinked right up, but he didn't hide away or deny it none.

"Yeah, I say we sit tight and rest up. Then we can decide what to do." Nodding, Preacher reached into his vest and pulled out a cheroot for the first time in a good bit, telling Hawk he was ready to relax.

Hawk leaned back upon his elbows, hat tipped low, watching the familiar sight of Preacher's lips wrapped around the smoke. There was just something about that man's mouth, and about the way the smoke's feeble light limned Preacher's face...made a man happy.

Hell, after the last little bit he could appreciate happy.

He got a companionable sort of 'me, too' smile from Preacher, those stiff shoulders letting go as Dime settled at the man's feet.

Bear made something like dumplings and stew and it was almost as fine as anything that widow woman'd made for them in her fancy dishes. They all sat right happy, even Bear and Abraham settled by having good food and a quiet night. And if either of them noticed when Preacher got up in the dark and wandered off, smoking, well...neither of them said.

Hawk noticed, though, and followed after a bit, nostrils flaring as he followed the scent of ash. Like each time before, he saw Preacher, just outlined against the sky, the glow of the cheroot pulling him. Preacher glanced over as he walked up, white teeth flashing.

"Howdy."

"Padre." He nodded, tipped his hat. Soon Preacher would offer him a smoke and they'd wander, boots quiet in the dust.

"Want a smoke?" Then the pattern broke just a bit when Preacher leaned in real quick to kiss him.

He kept their lips together, deepening the contact, drinking deep from that well. That mouth moved on his, Preacher's lips tasting like rain water and smoke, good and hot and full of hope. Yeah, that tasted like hope.

He reckoned he was lost and saved, all in one, so he wrapped his hand around Preacher's hip and held right on.

The cheroot hit the ground and Preacher grabbed onto him and held just as tight, kissing him silly. His hat went clean off, flying to the ground. It must mean something that he didn't even reach for it, just rubbed both their chests together like they was both sticks and he was looking to make fire.

"Hawk..." Preacher sounded wild, gone from happy to needy in nothin' flat, like a wild pony. Those hands clutched at him, one high on his back, the other low.

"Uh-huh." He nipped the padre's lip, then lifted his chin, baring his throat and begging for Preacher's attention.

"Mmm." Yeah, Preacher knew, and gave as freely as ever, kissing his scarred skin, licking at it, breath warm and moist. They were gonna be one man, they kept pushing that way. His breath came fast, the heat of Preacher's tongue easing aches he didn't remember having.

They turned in a slow circle, like both of them was looking for a place to light, and they neither of them found one, so they just sank down to their knees. He felt like he'd done this a hundred times before. So long as he could do it a hundred more times and a hundred times after that, Hawk reckoned he could handle it.

The ground rubbed hard under their knees, and Preacher pulled him down even more, stretching out to put one hand under his head, cushioning him. There, now. They could touch at their leisure that way.

He whispered into Preacher's mouth, words that weren't meant for the sunlight, but that his padre heard and understood, just like that. Padre seemed to know his heart and his skin, parting his clothes with a sure hand, fingers hot as blazes on his belly.

"So hot..." Maybe he felt just as warm to Preacher. It sure seemed so when they rubbed together, Preacher reaching under his trousers, fingers pushing at the fabric.

"Like a fire." His Johnson poked out, pushing toward Preacher's touch like a dowsing stick toward a spring. It caught the man's attention, too, and that rough hand closed around him, pulling at his prick like there was no tomorrow. He thought to worry when Preacher pulled away from his kiss, but then damned if the man didn't bend and put that mouth right above where his hand was...

Hawk's cry was sharp and needy, almost a bark of pure want. His hips rolling, bringing himself closer to that maddening damned mouth. Preacher sucked him, licking up and down, giving him so much. Too much. That mouth made him dance.

"Please. Please, Padre." Weren't another man on earth he'd beg. Not one.

There was not one damned bit of teasing as Preached gave him just what he needed. That mouth pulled at him, like yanking a sinner out of Hell and right into Heaven. And as he spent himself Preacher swallowed him right down, just like that.

His hands opened and closed on Preacher's shoulders, the ground beneath him seeming to sway. Oh. He. They.

Humming a jaunty tune, Preacher moved right up and kissed him, making the happiest noises a man could make. It all but made him chuckle. He could taste himself on Preacher's tongue - salt and bitter and odd, but still somehow right. He reached down, hand cupping Preacher's bulge and rubbing.

Damned if the man's eyes didn't roll back, Preacher rubbing frantically against his hand. "That's it. That's it..."

He tore open Preacher's placket, fingers holding tight, giving as much as he'd gotten. Preacher moaned and wriggled for him, thrusting up into his touch. That harsh sound spurred him on, making him go faster.

"Padre." He brought their mouths together, tongue pressing into Preacher's lips, tasting himself there.

"Mmm. Yeah." God that man could kiss, and oh, it was good. Real good, giving him shivers. Wasn't no shivering from Preacher, though. That man was hot as fire.

His hips began to move again, Hawk's cock half-filled and eager. His backside clenched as he pushed closer, body needing everything Preacher could give him.

"Hawk...Hawk, please. I just. Damn." It felt like a storm rising in Preacher's body, the tension in those muscles just ready to explode.

"Anything." The things Preacher made him think, made him want.

"Please." Thrashing, Preacher begged with voice and body for release.

He rolled Preacher's balls with one hand, tugged good and hard with the other, demanding that Preacher give it up for him. That was all it took. Preacher hollered good and loud, prick jerking in Hawk's hand, seed spilling out hot and musky.

He brought his hand up to his mouth, licking it clean, the flavor of Preacher sank down into his bones.

"Ohhh." The long, drawn out groan held a wealth of satisfaction. "Good deal."

"Yes. Good." He met Preacher's eyes, straight on. "I'll stay with you. Ride with you."

For as long as he could. As long as Preacher'd let him.

Chapter Thirteen

Preacher rolled over in his bedroll, looking at down at Hawk. Damn, the man was sleeping peaceful. Preacher hated to wake him. They'd had three days of peace and quiet. Now they had to move on, though. Had to. The storms were building up, and Preacher figured he knew just the place to go and weather them. He'd resisted it, because no man liked to feel like a bear cub who couldn't make it on his own in the woods, but it was time.

Time to go see Jett.

Sighing, he touched Hawk's shoulder, watching the man wake up.

Those blue eyes flashed open, staring up into his own. Hawk went from dead asleep to wide awake in seconds.

"Shhh. S'all right, Hawk. We need to get moving. Figured I'd wake you first."

"Storms are coming." The man's voice was barely there first thing in the morning.

"I know. I figured we'd head back toward the east. I got someone you need to meet. He can provision us, too."

"Meet?" It was sorta humbling, really. The way Hawk didn't reckon the idea was safe, but wouldn't let him go it alone.

"An old friend." Hell, Jett was so old Preacher wondered if he was still alive, but it was worth trying.

Hawk nodded as if it made perfect sense. "How far do we ride?"

"Well, we can make it in two, maybe three days. I think. I'm a little hazy on where we are." Smiling a little, Preacher shrugged.

Hawk chuckled, tilted his head toward the escarpment. "Near the river."

"Well, that much I know," he said, popping Hawk's bottom. "Not news."

Hawk started laughing, the rough, raw sound making him smile. He didn't hear it often enough.

"Uh huh. I bet Bear would know where the Hell we are." Bear could draw him out a map on the ground, get them headed in the right direction.

"Prob'ly. Them Injuns know about rivers and all." Was that a wink?

"They know a lot about a lot. Not as much about you, though. I think I know that." Preacher kissed Hawk, tracing that smile with his tongue.

"No one knows as much about me as you do, no matter what's said."

That gave him a savage sense of satisfaction. That feller that had been so hard to handle, well, he may think he knew Hawk, he may even have had him, but Preacher loved

Hawk, and figured he had Hawk's love in return. That meant more than any other bond.

Their eyes met and locked, the black centers of Hawk's eyes suddenly big and deep, a hint of fire in the center of them.

Fire.

Lord.

Preacher wasn't sure whether to pull back or move up to kiss that right out of his sight. Chills ran down his spine. "Hawk?"

"Yeah, Padre?" Brimstone. He could smell it. He *knew* he could.

"I do love you, Mister." Kissing seemed his best option. That made him forget all sorts of shit.

Hawk opened up to him, moving them farther away from the fire and away from eyes, if anyone woke up.

Yeah, he could handle that. He went happily, arms going around Hawk as they settled. Warm and heavy against him, Hawk no longer smelled like brimstone. Now he was all man.

Those long hands dragged on down his sides, heading down to his hips, thumbs pushing in and rubbing in circles. So close to his Johnson, but not touching. Not giving him what he needed. His hips arched right up, his body trying to get what it wanted. He just had to get in the right place, get Hawk to stop teasing.

Hawk sure didn't make it easy for him, though, fingers brushing his sacs, his hipbones, his thighs.

Grunting, Preacher moved, pushing and pushing, wanting more. His damned lip hurt where he was biting off words Bear or Abraham might hear, and he finally reached down and moved Hawk's hand to close around him.

"Preacher." Hawk's hand echoed his own touch, those fingers finally touching him where he needed, rubbing him as if to set him afire.

"Yes. God, please." Like flame, that touch licked at him, sending him groaning and biting at Hawk's skin. His prick just jumped, throbbing.

His placket was opened, his prick pushing up against Hawk's, both their skins seeming to be on fire.

"Just like that." All he could do was thrust and pull back, the friction making him gasp. He might well go to Hell for this some day, but he couldn't care.

"Yes." They were leaking and desperate, hands clinging and grasping at each other as their hips jerked and rolled. They kissed deep, both of them making muffled noises behind the contact, both of them trying to hold it back. Preacher's eyes rolled, the pleasure almost too much, too good.

One of Hawk's hands cupp
fingertips tapping behind, ligh
behind his eyelids. His whole
hard, and Preacher held on to l
pulled, riding out the pleasure t
him. He shook with it, and he tl
was gonna kill him.

Hawk tumbled right on behind, gasping and
grunting against his mouth as heat joined his
own, spreading against his skin.

"Well, good morning." There was
something about being out under the open
sky...with the storm clouds. Damn it. "We
need to move."

Hawk's eyes shot upward and he got a
short, quick nod. "Yup. Saddle up. We'll eat a
cold breakfast."

That sounded ominous. Hell, he knew it
was. He could see, couldn't he? Grumbling,
Preacher levered up and offered Hawk a hand.
"I'll get Bear, tell him not to build up the fire."

Hawk hauled himself up, that damn Fred
right there, dancing and tossing his head like
whatever was on the air was talking to him.

"You'll see to the horses?" It was just a
courtesy to ask. He knew Hawk would. The
man took good care of all the horses, saddle
and tack.

"I will." Hawk ran one hand through his
hair, the act seeming to throw sparks out in the
air.

His skin felt too tight, like all the water in him was burning off. Preacher panted, tugging on clothes while he trotted to wake up Abraham and Bear, get them moving. Dime hopped after him, barking and fussing, just letting them and anything in earshot know something wasn't the way it ought to be.

Damn. He felt like they ought to be running, not just hurrying, and he kicked Bear out of bed, reaching for Abraham's shoulder.

"Come on, you lot. Up. We gotta git."

Abraham blustered, but Bear shot up like, well, like he'd been shot at, braid bouncing on the broad back. Hawk got them all loaded up, Fred dancing and circling the whole damn time.

Abraham was still half asleep when they rode out, all of them spurring into a lope, that little donkey managing a sharp trot and braying all the way. They needed to get out from under this cloud. No damned good would come of it.

Hawk pushed them from behind, whooping and popping their pack mules when they wanted to falter. The rain and wind started behind them, the thunder booming out loud enough to shake the ground.

Then it was on them, the rain turning to hail as it hit them, the round, icy balls as solid as rocks, pelting them hard. Their horses slipped and slid, panicky, their eyes rolling. Only Fred and Dime kept them going, that crazy horse pushing with his nose, Dime nipping at the horses' hooves.

"Padre! We can't outrun it. We gotta hole up, somewhere high." Hawk's voice rang out, the words ending in a grunt as a chunk of ice hit that black hat.

Preacher wheeled his mount, searching the terrain, making sure Hawk was still upright on his horse. "There!" That outcropping of rock had to be big enough.

Fred nearly screamed, hooves pounding the air before running the direction of his finger.

They'd almost made it when Abraham went down, his donkey's scream not a bit like Fred's. No this was pure fear and pure flashing hooves and teeth and then Abraham was down, not even a sound coming from the man as he slid down the side of the rock face.

Hawk wheeled around, Fred's hooves slip-sliding on the mud as the man headed for the spot where Abraham fell.

"Hawk!" He hated that he called for Hawk first, since Abraham had been with him almost from the beginning, but he'd never claimed to be anything but weak.

"Stay, Padre." Hawk looked back at him, eyes blazing under the black brim of that hat.

"But..." Shit. Preacher nodded, set to helping Bear with the pack horse. That was all he could do now.

Hawk and Fred disappeared and he'd be damned if the clouds didn't go from gray to sheer black, just like Hawk'd set off something in the sky.

Preacher finally remembered how to pray. He prayed long and hard while he tried to get everyone he could in from the storm, and if it was guilt that had him putting Abraham first this time, so be it.

The rain smashed into the ground, the sound like slaps upon bare skin that just barely hid the sounds of growling and snarling, the rough voice of evil that seemed to be hiding right up under the storm clouds. He settled the critters, then headed toward the ledge, stopping only when Bear's hand fell on his arm.

Preacher turned, gently, not wanting to fight. "I have to, Bear. I have to help him. He's...well. You got eyes and ears, even if you ain't got a tongue. You know what he is to me."

Bear looked at him, eyes dark and unhappy and whatever Bear mighta been thinking, they both turned when Abraham was pushed up over the ledge. He saw Hawk, soaking wet and grey under that tan, holding on to the wet rock, the mud pouring down over him. Preacher and Bear both went out at a dead run, heading out just in time to see something - something clawed and vicious and wrong - grabbing Hawk's shoulder, digging into the meat and yanking him down.

"No!" Preacher screamed it, reaching for his gun and coming up empty. Damn, but he needed to start carrying again. He ran harder, thinking as fast as he could, shouting prayers at the same time.

His boots slid on the wet rock, and he damn near went over, going down onto his belly instead. The rain splashed up into his face - and later, he'd swear it was a blessing - blurring the writhing mass of flesh and fur and fang that was swirling at the bottom of the escarpment. What he could see were dozens of red eyes, glowing like the lit end of a cheroot.

That and Hawk, bleeding, gasping, dragging himself away from the swirl of madness, one painful bit at a time.

His body froze for one awful moment, self-preservation keeping him from moving. Then he moved, his body slipping and sliding, his hands and boot heels digging in to keep him moving toward Hawk.

Hawk lifted his head, those eyes staring up at him, blue as the winter sky.

He could see Bear out of the corner of his eye, pulling Abraham away from where Hawk had tossed him, letting him know that was all settled. Then he put all his attention on Hawk, looking right into those eyes while he held out a hand.

He swore he could see it all right there in Hawk's eyes - defeat and fear, exhaustion and pain and that thing that they had together. It was all right there as Hawk fought to keep on, to reach out for him.

Sliding down a few more feet, Preacher scrabbled, trying to catch a hold. He wasn't willing to give up either. Not on Hawk. Not now. His fingertips brushed Hawk's, setting his heart to pounding.

Lightning flashed and the rain came harder, Hawk's groan audible, even over the thunder, as the soil under Hawk let loose, the man sliding back a ways. "You gotta run, Padre."

"No. Not without you." Implacable, he grunted, pulling at Hawk and trying to back away from the edge of the canyon. "Come on. Come on, Hawk, help me."

"Cussed fool." Hawk's eyes flashed when the lightning did.

"Yes." His other hand closed on Hawk's collar so he could yank. "Come on. Hawk."

The rain couldn't completely obscure what was coming for them now, the heaving mass of bodies and snapping teeth making his head swim. No man should see that. No sir. It made his stomach roil, made his cheeks go hot, then cold. Clammy.

"Pray. You gotta. Back 'em down." Hawk managed to get his feet under him just enough to make a massive push, collapsing against him.

Preacher stared at Hawk for a moment, lying on his back where Hawk had sent them, arms tight around that wet, hard body. Then as the unearthly howls escalated, he threw Hawk off of him and rose to his knees, clasping his hands and beginning to pray.

Hawk disappeared from beside him, those icy eyes holding his for a long second before claws and fangs surrounded the man and left nothing but his own screams and a blood-streaked hand print on the stone.

Chapter Fourteen

Bear came for him, hauling him, still praying, back into the cave.

Praise god, Fred was there, screaming and stamping, pelt scarred and covered in blood.

"We need to see to Fred, Bear." Abraham was out cold, and Abraham's mount...well, that poor donkey was a loss, he guessed. Preacher unclenched his hands and looked around, hunting Dime, wanting to know they were all together.

They were. Dime was whining and lapping the blood from his own shoulder and leg.

The world grayed out at the edges for a minute, his body slumping a bit. Then a ringing slap rocked his head, forcing his eyes to pop right open. Bear grunted at him and slapped him again before pointing out the mouth of the cave.

Right. Hawk. He needed to get Hawk. Needed to get the others safe so he could...

His stomach rolled, and for a moment he craved the burn of whiskey, but Preacher held it together. He couldn't think about more than one thing at a time, couldn't let himself think about Hawk yet. Abraham first. Preacher scrabbled over to kneel beside Bear, looking down as Abraham began to stir.

Abraham was blinking and swaying some, but the man was there in those dazed eyes, staring over at him with something between fear and awe. "Hawk. Hawk did. I. Hawk. Hawk."

That weird-assed English accent got louder and louder, Little Bear staring at Abraham like the man was loco.

"Abraham? Are you all right, mister? You look tore up a bit."

"Did you see..." Those watery blue eyes rolled, the panic just kept at bay. "Did you *see*?"

"I didn't see much, no. Enough to scare me spitless..." He touched Abraham's shoulder. "Where does it hurt?"

"I. I don't believe I know. Hawk. He rode down. He rode *into* them."

"You're going to have to let me look." As gentle as he could, he turned Abraham this way and that. The man's clothes were soaked with more blood than the man had lost, and he flinched, knowing it was Hawk's blood.

There were dozens of little cuts - bites and scratches, tiny tears in Abraham's skin. It damn near looked like something'd thought about flaying the man. Had maybe made a good start on it and been interrupted.

Lord almighty. He started washing Abraham down, using water Bear brought, soothing each cut and raw spot. His whole body wanted to go and find Hawk, but Preacher ignored the urge.

Bear put a hand on his arm, and when he looked into those black, black eyes he saw everything he was thinking. Preacher nodded.

"We got to get Abraham to Jett's, Bear. Then I swear I'm coming back for him, I swear. I'll go to Hell itself. They can't have him." He stared out into the storm that still raged for a moment, the rain coming down in sheets and hiding the world. "They just can't."

Chapter Fifteen

He knew it wasn't a dream this time because of the smell.

Nothing smelled so much like Hell on Earth as this. He could hear the screams, the cries of people falling to the dogs all around him, and all he could do was hope that those screams belonged to strangers, to the willing, to the greedy.

Not to his Preacher.

He'd've prayed, if he knew how, but he'd never talked to Preacher's god – not before, when that god was his enemy or after, when all he could wonder was why any god would let beings like him roam the land and hunt. So he didn't pray, didn't waste his breath.

But he wished, real hard, balls to bones, that Preacher made it through. Preacher and Fred and all them, 'cause they was his family, his own.

His skin crackled and blistered where clawed fingers dug into him, those red eyes burning into him. "You did not believe you would escape me?"

Of course he had believed. If he had not believed, he would never have run the first time. He was afflicted with hope.

"Aquilon. You are a fool."
He didn't reckon that had changed.

***

It took a damned eternity to find Jett.

The old man wasn't where Preacher had thought he would be, and they had to wander around too damned long to get to him. The man had moved his little farm way on out. By the time they got there, Abraham had gotten a fever, Bear kept grunting, Fred kept whinnying, and Preacher was about to go out of his mind taking care of them all.

They finally made it, though. The little cabin was neat as a pin, the approach cleared out so Jett could see who was coming, and probably so the man could shoot anyone he didn't want to see.

"Well, we ain't dead yet," Preacher said. "So I'll go knock."

Bear grunted and waved a hand before making the motion of a shooting gun and a man running. Yeah. He'd duck if Jett came out a'shooting.

"Will do." Moseying on up nice and easy, even though every urge told him to run, Preacher knocked on the door, and damned if it didn't swing right open, the smell of cheroot smoke coming out along with a rough old voice.

"Come on in, boy. Been expecting you."

A big old crow fluttered to the ground, raucous as it screamed at them all, Dime most of all. The horses shifted, but Dime bounded up, growling and barking, telling that bird what-for. It even made Bear chuckle. Hell, Preacher'd swear that damned Fred chuffed.

"Well, I guess y'all should take that as a sign." Jett came on out the door, shotgun up on one shoulder as he looked them over. "Good to see you, Virgil. Howdy, Bear. Looks like you picked you up a few new riders."

Preacher nodded. "We did. Abraham is the pale one, there, and that's Fred, the wonder horse. I need your help."

Jett nodded, even as Bear started unloading the pack mules. "Well, you're all welcome."

Preacher crawled down to the ground, moving like an old man.

"Lord, Virgil. What'd you get yourself into?"

"I'll tell you, but only if I can do it while you patch me up so I can ride out again. We had to leave a man behind. Bear, can you see to Abraham?" They limped inside, Jett mumbling about bandages and liquor, and Preacher could feel his body yearning toward that damned bottle, but he stayed on the other side of the room.

He needed a clear head, damn it.

"So where did you leave this feller?" Jett asked, breaking him out of his thoughts.

"At the canyon about a quarter day's ride from here. Looks like a crescent moon."

"You'll need food, then. I got some beans with some salt pork. It's gonna be a hard ride, Virgil." Those too old eyes looked right into his, as if asking him if he wanted to make this choice.

"I can't leave him, Jett. He's...well, he ain't all I got, but he's all I need."

"Then we'll go. Get you a bowl of them beans and some hard tack. Time's a'wastin'."

The food tasted like sawdust in his mouth, but Preacher ate, knowing he had to have some reserve of strength. Bear moved about, tending to Abraham. Jett went outside to get them some horses saddled up, and Preacher watched his hands shake like he was just off the bottle and not years gone.

Fighting the food that tried to come back up, Preacher rose, going to clasp Bear's shoulder. The Indian looked up and Preacher met his eyes.

"If we don't come back, you know what to do."

A harsh noise of denial came from Bear, and Preacher summoned up a smile. "I know, Bear. But you got to promise me that much."

A solemn nod was his reply.

"Good man."

Bear would see to it if they fell in battle. He'd salt the ground, say the prayers for their souls. He'd see Abraham well and settled.

That was all there was to it.

Jett had come in without him seeing, and was watching him when he turned toward the door.

"You ready, son?"

"Yessir."

Jett grinned suddenly, that crinkled old face splitting wide. "Just like old times, huh? Come on, boy. Let's ride."

Chapter Sixteen

Aquilon. He will kill you, you know this? Come with us. Rejoin the pack and we will lick your wounds.

Hawk knew that voice, that soft whisper. His second, Lanisto. They had been compatriots once, had run together for hours, biting and howling and hunting. They had been created together, Carchion forming them together from clay and fire, breathing them into life with that fetid breath.

That's right. We are brothers. You were not meant for this, Aquilon. To be bound and tied here when there is flesh to feast upon. You were meant for better things and the little witch confused you. He could feel Lanisto's breath on his cheek, the hot, lumpy brush of the hound's tongue collecting the salt and blood from his skin. *You would spread for the human, would you? Allow him to mount you like a bitch?*

He growled, a red rage building inside. *You are not worthy to consider him.*

The bite to his jaw was quick, sharp, a fire raging within him and he pulled violently at the ropes at his wrists.

*He was right. You are a human. Filthy and
hairless. Weak. I could snap your balls clean
off, eat them and make you watch as you
scream.* Lanisto padded down, tongue scraping
against his side, his thigh.

Then that slick, slimy tongue touched his
privates; the bile rising in his throat.

Hawk closed his eyes against the horror of
it, remembering his Preacher. Laughing.
Riding. Preaching. That cheroot shining cherry
red in the night and leading him home. That
first day by the river, water clean and sweet in
his mouth, Preacher's lips open against him.

To see that again, to see that sorry son of a
bitch again, Hawk'd pray.

Goddamnit.

A sheer fury mixed with horror filled the
air, teeth snapping hard in the air above him.
He was too shocked to scream, just stared as
the hound whimpered, stumbling away from
him.

Please. Please, let them be safe. Let me see
him again.

"Stop it." Carchion was right there,
whapping him with a stick, over and over.
"Stop that. Stop it now. You can't *do* this.
You're mine! Mine!"

Hawk managed to smile, the memory of
Preacher sunk down into his skin.

Please let Preacher be safe. Let that ornery
bastard know I was his.

Chapter Seventeen

They tried to leave Fred behind, injured as he was, but the damned, mule-headed beast insisted on going, rearing and biting when Jett tried to calm him enough to tie him in the little lean to.

Preacher didn't blame him. Every minute that they stayed was a minute that Hawk might be dying, all at once or in slow degrees. Jett had that quiet, focused intensity that meant he was on the trail, and Preacher was praying like he'd never prayed in his life as he spurred his horse on, trying to reach that damned canyon that led right to the mouth of Hell.

They heard it before they saw it, and the smell of Hellfire had their horses screaming and rearing, only Fred staying calm, running back and forth at the top of the scree.

"We won't surprise them," Jett said when they finally pulled up, the storm on them in a fury of lightning and thunder so loud Preacher could barely hear.

"Then what the Hell do we do?" he shouted, his hands clenching and unclenching as an unearthly howl greeted them.

"You sure your man ain't lost already?" The old preacher grabbed hold of his hat as the wind gusted, Fred pawing the ground and looking to run down there right into the thick of things.

No. No, Hawk wasn't lost. Not yet, damn it.

"I'd know. I swear, Jett, I can hear him in my mind. Calling to me. Praying for me..." Praying for him. Oh, God in Heaven, Hawk was praying. He knew it.

"Well, then. I reckon we'd best go fetch him. Good Lord protects his own, praise Jesus." Then Jett sorta nodded once to Fred, who screamed out in answer. "You get up on Fred there and you don't look at them things. You don't talk to them. You ride down and get you your man."

"And you? What the Hell are you gonna do, Jett?"

"Son." He got a grin, wild and damn near joyous, which given the situation scared the tarnation out of him. "I reckon to create one Hell of a diversion."

Well, Hell. He'd have to trust in that. He got up on Fred, patting that bloody neck. "You and me, you stubborn nag. Just you and me. Don't you fall, you hear me?"

Fred snorted and he'd swear somewhere in the back of his mind he heard a growly, old voice telling him to shut up and hold on, Hawk needed him.

Hawk was praying on him.

Then they started down, right where the storm was raging.

The wind howled, and the rain turned to hail the minute he started down in, pounding at him, tearing at his clothes. Goddamn, he could hear Fred screaming, knew every step was agony, but they plunged right down, just like he imagined Hawk doing for Abraham. He almost lost his seat, but righted himself just in time, clinging to Fred's neck.

Hawk was right there, in the eye of it all. Bloodied and broke and bound on a stone, but the storm couldn't touch him, just swirled around him as his lips moved. Fred bucked and reared, hooves connecting with fur before the damned nag leapt, landing right there beside Hawk, pushing toward the man's light.

It near broke his heart, to see Hawk praying, keeping those furious beasts at bay, when he hadn't even thought to add his own prayers to the mix. Preacher did, then, raising his voice just like he did in a tent meeting, hearing it ring out loud and clear.

"Lord, save us from these Devils!" he shouted, reaching down for Hawk, willing those bonds to break. "We've walked into the fire for you, Lord. You gave him to me, I see that now. I'm not ready for you to take him. Please, God, help me take him home."

Those blue eyes opened then, staring at him, his Hawk right there and, praise God, them old ropes started unraveling, the storm backing farther and farther away.

Fred leaned his big old head down, those wicked sharp teeth helping the good Lord and their faith out. Hawk was groaning, eyes rolling like dice as those poor hurt arms tried to move, to wrap around Fred's neck.

There wasn't a stitch of clothing left to pull on, so Preacher had to lean too far, too much to grab ahold of Hawk's back, but something unseen kept his ass in the saddle, something answering his prayer, and he hauled with all of his strength. Hawk slipped and slid, hot blood running on the man's skin, but Preacher wasn't gonna let go, no sir. Not now.

"Come on, Lord. Just one more push..."

"Preacher." Hawk's smile could light up the darkest night, and they got that push, Hawk slick and burning against him, body slumped against Fred.

"Virgil! Son! You quit lollygagging down there now! It's time to ride!" Jett's voice got to him, along with the screaming of the horses.

"Yessir." Holding Hawk tighter than any treasure, Preacher turned Fred toward the top of the rise, prayers falling off his lips.

A surging mass of bodies sat between them and where they needed to be, flames seeming to lick at the feet and muzzles of what had to be the damned hounds of Hell. No man should be faced with that sight and stay sane, but he did it for Hawk.

His man. His.

"Now would be a good time for that distraction, old man!" he hollered, putting most of the last of his strength into being heard.

The words had barely left his mouth when the words of the 23rd Psalm seemed to echo through the canyon, Jett's voice rolling louder than his ears could hear.

The Lord is my Shepherd; I shall not want.

The rocks started trembling, shaking like the earth liked to open up and swallow them whole.

He maketh me to lie down in green pastures:
He leadeth me beside the still waters.

The demon dogs started howling, chasing them, driving them straight toward the rock face.

He restoreth my soul:
He leadeth me in the paths of righteousness for His name's sake.

Fred reared, damn near losing them, but the horse started climbing, hooves sparking on the black stone.

Hawk's head rolled, eyes showing nothing but white, but those lips were moving, praying. Saying that psalm along with Jett like he'd been washed in the blood.

Yea, though I walk through the valley of the shadow of death,
I will fear no evil: For thou art with me;

Hawk's fingers squeezed him, held on.

They broke the top of the canyon wall like Fred had become that winged horse of myth, Preacher's lips recounting the prayer right along. Hell, for all he knew the damned *horse* was praying. Jett was there, the horses trembling and bucking, and the old man didn't even spare them a glance, just wheeled and made for the plains like his ass was on fire.

Holding Hawk close, knowing they weren't safe yet, Preacher did the same, begging Fred for one more burst of speed.

They made it to the riverbank, Fred not even stopping at the edge of the Pecos, just forging in and driving through like the damned river weren't deep enough to drown them all and fast enough to sweep them to Mexico.

"Come on, damn it. Come on. Just the other side." Oh, Lord, they were gonna die. He could feel the undertow pulling at them, and Preacher just buried his face in Hawk's neck and asked God for one more favor. He'd save souls until doomsday for this one man.

Just this one.

The water pulled at them, weighed them down, and he could hear Jett cussing and whipping and threatening the nags.

"Come on, you lot. You want them critters to eat your sorry asses? No. No, I didn't reckon. Y'all move. Swim, God damn you! Swim!"

"Hawk. Hawk, help me...tell Fred he's gotta get to the bank."

It wasn't selfish to ask. It wasn't just because he wanted to hear Hawk's voice. Fred was failing and nothing Preacher did was urging the horse on.

Hawk groaned, head tossing, then those blue eyes fastened on him. Saw him.

"Don't stop. 'Mon Fred. 'Mon now. We cain't stop now, you and me. We cain't let that lying bastard win."

Whether it was the words or the way Hawk pushed Fred's nose above the water or sheer dumb luck, Preacher'd never know.

All he knew was that horse surged up and did it, collapsing on the bank, chest heaving.

They all lay there for long moments, the sound of Fred's wheezing terrible to hear. Then Jett was beside them, soaked to the skin, water pouring off his hat in sheets.

"Love to give y'all time to rest, but we ain't got it. Come on, now, get on up on the horse that brung you. We'll drag the other'n if we have to."

How much farther could they go without losing Hawk and Fred both? Preacher struggled to his feet, tossing his head to try and clear it.

He grabbed Hawk up off the ground, cringing at the dead weight of the man. "Help me, Jett."

The old man spurred right over and yanked Hawk right up off the ground, those poor, torn feet just a'dangling. Then he plopped Hawk on horseback.

"Come on, son, get up here and hold him. I'll see to the other."

His body screamed at him when he pulled himself up behind Hawk, holding on for dear life. Behind him he heard Jett calling out, pushing Fred to rise, and it was the strangest thing he ever did hear.

"Get yer ass up, you stubborn old fool," Jett shouted. "Get up! I ain't a'gonna leave you here, you flea bitten son of a whore, you hear me?"

He heard Fred's weak whinny and then Jett's voice broke. "No, sir. No, I don't think so. You get yer skinny butt up right now. You cain't leave it now!"

That silly nag got up, too, and followed them, stumbling like a newborn foal. Thank God. Preacher didn't know if he could leave Fred behind, and now he didn't have to make the choice.

The dogs either couldn't or wouldn't cross the river, so they managed to leave the barking and howling behind, the horses calming the farther they went. Finally Jett whistled up a stop. "We gotta get him patched, boy, if we're gonna save him."

Preacher sorta reckoned Hawk'd done got himself saved, just fine.

Chapter Eighteen

The fire Jett managed to get going smoked like mad, but Preacher wasn't worried none about anything finding them. He was worried about Hawk, and getting a shelter up to cover the man while he looked at those wounds.

Those hundreds of wounds.

Preacher almost fell into despair over how bad Hawk looked once the slicker and the half rotten tree branch made a lean to. Almost. But the look in Hawk's eyes back at the river kept him going, kept his hands moving and his lips working like a child reciting Bible verses.

Jett worked just as hard on Fred, the man singing to that damn horse and treating the critter like it was a person, doctoring them nasty bite wounds and packing the worst ones.

He got Hawk turned over so he could look at that poor back. Lord have mercy, the man was all but flayed. Preacher took a cloth Jett had given him, dipping it in the water they'd gathered, stroking it as gently as he could over the torn spots.

Hawk moaned, all raw and low, fingers scrabbling at the ground as the man tried to pull away from him.

"Shhh. Hush now. I got you." How many times had he said that in the last hour? How many times had he had to hurt Hawk to help him?

"They didn't get you." Hawk eased up some. He'd heard that, too. The way Hawk'd worried over him and Fred, Bear, and even Abraham. "They wanted you and they didn't get you. Didn't hurt you. Didn't take you with them."

"No, sir. And Fred is right over there, getting patched up. Bear and Abraham are safe. You just got to let me clean you up, honey." Every scrape filled him with a mixture of rage and relief.

"They made promises, you know? Liars. All of them. Lies and lies..."

"They were. Just trying to weaken you. Just trying to wear you down." Hawk never flinched when Preacher hit the worst of the big lumps on the back of his neck and head, now that he was awake.

"Cain't go back to what I was." Hawk turned his head, blinked over. "It burns in me, Padre. It burns all over."

"Shhh." Poor Hawk. What lies had those monsters told him, spouted at him while they beat him? "You're riding with me now. You're not backsliding anywhere."

"No. I ain't sliding. I ain't his. I paid and paid..." Hawk started moaning, mumbling, the

words not making a lick of sense, all just
wandering and worrying.

Jett came over, face grey as winter and
shook his head. "Horse'll make it. How about
your man?"

"I...I don't know. He's awake." That had to
be a good sign. Had to. "You hanging in?"

"Yessir. That's some powerful evil out
there." Jett looked Hawk over, shook his head.
"He's got himself a light, don't he?"

"He does. I think I needed him, Jett. Think I
was getting a little lost." He stroked Hawk's
hair, watching his hand as it slid over the short
locks.

"I'm thinking he was more than a little lost,
once upon a time. You know what he was?"

Preacher closed his eyes. "I know he was
with them things, Jett. I ain't no fool. But he
ain't now. Not now."

"No. No, if'n he was one of them, you'd
not've brung him out. He suffered something
powerful and still kept his faith."

"He did." Preacher loved Hawk all the more
for it. His fingers tested one of the scrapes
down the back of Hawk' arms. Damn.

"I'll make some vittles; see if you can get
tea in him. We've gone too far to lose him
now."

"Yessir." Jett had been his savior once,
pulling him out of his own pit of despair. He
didn't want to be Hawk's savior, or have Hawk

be his. He just wanted them stronger together than they were apart.

Jett clapped him once on the back. "Have faith, son. The good Lord ain't forsook you yet."

"Doesn't look like it." Going back to his tending, Preacher stroked Hawk's head, soothing after each sting. "Doesn't look like it at all."

No. No, he had Hawk here with him, and that evil bastard was raging on the other side of the water. God was with him.

Preacher'd just have to take it on faith that He'd stay.

Chapter Nineteen

The burn and itch was bone deep, making him twist and groan and reach for...

Something.

Anything.

Sometimes the night was filled with red eyes, sometimes the sun burned away everything but the touch of wet cloths on his skin.

And sometimes warm, rough hands cradled him while a deep, low voice told him to hush, that he was fine, Preacher had him.

Padre.

Oh.

He shifted toward that voice, hands reaching up to touch.

"That's it," Preacher said, sounding a long ways away. The touch came a lot closer, soft as those hard hands could be.

His mouth opened and closed, but it was dry as dust and damned if his tongue didn't just flap uselessly.

"Oh, now, I bet you need some of this." Cool water slid right across his parched tongue to trickle down his throat, soothing the terrible itch.

"Uhn." He moaned and nodded, lips open for more. He swore to God he could hear the water hitting his belly.

Preacher gave him more in a slow, steady stream, just enough for him to swallow. The man just seemed to know.

He hunted up a smile for Preacher, or tried to, his lips cracking with the effort. "Th. Thank you."

"You're welcome." Preacher bent and kissed his mouth, lips cool and damp, easing him. "Glad you waited on me, mister."

"Had to. Couldn't let them win." Couldn't lose himself yet.

"Nope. You should have seen those bastards, Hawk. Should have seen the way they cowered when you prayed." Preacher sounded proud. So proud.

He wasn't sure what that meant, that Preacher's god would come for one like him. Wasn't sure at all, but he'd take it. "You came. I was hoping for you."

"Always come for you." That hand stroked over his head like it had all night and who knew how much of the day. "We're gonna have to ride soon..."

"Tie me to the saddle." He couldn't hold himself up, not yet anyway, but he wouldn't hold them back.

"I will, as soon as you're able. And Fred. He's poorly, but Jett's been dosing him."

Footsteps sounded, and Preacher looked away from him, back over Preacher's shoulder.

Dark eyes looked down at him, into him. "Look at you. You're awake."

He nodded, groaning as the action made the world swim.

"No trying to move, son," the old man said. "We'll get you rigged up so you can ride, but you need to conserve strength."

"Where're we going?" They'd be coming for him. He could feel it in his bones, that fury and hungry.

"To my home, son. It's solid."

Preacher smiled down at him, nodding. "It's a good place. I swear."

So long as they were going together and taking Fred. "We gotta get in afore the storms come. They'll find us, given time."

"Yup." The old man sounded almost...cheerful. "Fred's ready to go. Get the stuff ready to lash him to the horse, Virgil."

Virgil?

He cracked an eye, looked at Preacher.

He got a slight grin, the crinkles around Preacher's eyes pulling up. "S'my given name. Here, have some more water before I go get ready."

"No wonder you go by Preacher." He caught himself staring, just watching that smile like a newborn fool.

"Uh huh. I get a sight less teasing."
Bending, Preacher gave him another watery
kiss. "You hang in there. Be back in a flash."

He nodded again, swallowing against the
pain. It was time to ride. Time to go in away
from the storm.

Chapter Twenty

It took another whole day to get them back
to the cabin, but they made it in, Bear and
Abraham waiting on them, both looking drawn
and worried.

It took both him and Jett to get Hawk off
Fred's saddle where they had the man tied.
Just the look of those marks had Abraham
retching, but Bear's lips only tightened like
he'd seen it all before, and that damn Injun
took Fred's reins to get the poor thing settled.

"Come on, Hawk. Inside. You gotta." They
kept the man moving, sorta half-carrying, half-
dragging him. Dime set to barking, then
pushed right up to Hawk, whining and
whimpering.

"Yeah. Yeah, pup. We know. Let's get him
settled." Jett looked over at Abraham, scowled.
"Quit your fussing and come make a pallet. He
needs a rest."

Hawk stumbled in, gone to a worn sleep
before they got him laid out on the pallet.

Abraham came easier, settling against the
wall with a sigh and a tired smile. "Quite nice
to meet you while I'm awake, Mister Jett."

"And you. Looks like y'all fought the good
fight," Jett said, looking Abraham over as well.

"You want to pour me some whiskey? Lord knows the Preacher here doesn't keep the stuff."

"I believe I could use a nip, as well." Abraham offered Jett a nod, even as Bear snorted, rolled his eyes at Jett. Preacher'd met up with Bear during his long stay with Jett and the Injun and sky pilot seemed to communicate just fine. "I do appreciate it."

"Not at all." Some of Jett's finer upbringing came up in those words, that old, gray head just a'nodding. One gnarled finger pointed at Hawk. "Think he could use a nip?"

Preacher studied Hawk, then shook his head. "I think he just needs rest."

"What about you, son? What do you need?"

Hawk's eyes flew open at Jett's words, one strong hand wrapping around Jett's wrist. "He don't drink no more."

Jett stared down at Hawk and it looked like it wasn't just Bear who could speak on another level. Jett just coughed out a hard laugh and nodded. "I know, boy. I got coffee and I got water, and some grub."

"Good." Hawk's hand hit the hard-pack with a thud, icy eyes rolling back into the man's head. Lord have mercy.

Jett, though? He just threw his head back and hooted.

"He's really quite something," Abraham said, nodding his chin at Hawk. "Amazing, in fact."

"Amazing?" A jug was handed to Abraham, a kettle put over the fire to heat. Jett was as spry as any young man, hadn't seemed to age a bit in the years since Preacher'd ridden off to do the Lord's bidding.

"Indeed. He pulled me right out of the pit of Hell, I vow."

Preacher suddenly needed a smoke, and he went to roll one, standing in the doorway and looking out over Jett's land.

One hand landed on his shoulder, Bear sliding out to finish caring for the horses. Fred wandered over to the door, big head pushing in and staring, first at Hawk, then Jett.

Preacher snorted and pushed the horse out of the way. "He'll be fine. Come on, now, and let me out so I can have my damned cheroot."

Damned if that horse didn't steal the smoke right out of his fingers, dancing back and whinnying.

"You eat my tobacco and I'll beat you half dead, you mangy mule." He started out after Fred, ready to just go on a tear.

Fred snorted, head bobbing, tempting him farther out, horsey breath blowing over his tobacco.

"You rotten sumbitch." Bone tired as he was, he still leaped right out and ran for his tobacco, batting at Fred's nose.

Fred bucked up a bit, tossed the tobacco into the air. Ornery cuss.

"Now, come on. I ain't playing no more. Come on and give it back." All he wanted was a smoke. Just to ease his bones.

Fred stopped, stared, heavy chin landing on his shoulder, just like he'd seen it do to Hawk, over and over.

"He approves of you. You ought to be pleased." Jett sure sounded that way.

"Should I?" With one hand he rescued his bag of smoke, and with the other he reached up to scratch Fred's ears. "He's special enough, that's for sure."

"He's here for a reason, I vow." Jett leaned back, one eyebrow lifting. "You got one Hell of a story for me, son, now that we're settled in."

"I do, Jett. Worse than my last one, I tell you." His last hard case had been him, and Jett had cracked him pretty easily, drying him out and showing him the error of his ways before handing off the old, wide-brimmed preacher's hat and telling him he was ordained.

"You always were ambitious, Virgil, but this is bigger than I thought even you would try."

"Hell, I didn't know I was. I... I do worry I brought it on myself. There was this town." The town Abraham couldn't see. The town that no longer existed.

"Did you find him there, your Hawk?"

"No, sir. He came out of the dark one night a good way before that." And they had taken their best moments in the dark since then.

"Does he know what he is?" The tobacco shook in his fingers, the paper crackling as he stared over at Jett.

"I don't... I guess he has an idea now and again." The look on Hawk's face when that feller had appeared... yeah, he thought Hawk knew. Hell, Hawk knew more than he did. "I'm in over my head, Jett, and I don't know what to do. He thinks he ain't no good."

"Well, son. You just gotta have faith." Jett laughed and winked, took the tobacco pouch and rolled one. "You prayed over him?"

"Not yet." Lord, he'd been sort of... well. Ashamed. Scared to. Because of what they'd done. "It's been complicated."

"What all isn't? You got more complications than a two-tailed cat in a room of looms."

"I know it." That had him laughing, stroking Fred's nose. "Anyhoo, I need to sit and pray on it a bit, huh? Can I smoke first, Fred? Can I?"

That horse did *not* just nod like it understood him.

Shaking his head, he nodded at Jett. "Can you keep an eye on them? I won't be far, but I need to know they're safe to be able to think. You understand?"

"You're safe here. God watches over this place." There was a pure faith there, a belief that was deeper than anything Preacher'd ever known.

"I thank you for that, Jett. I truly do." He'd smoke, he'd think, and then he'd pray. And hopefully soon enough he'd have an answer as to what they had to do next.

Chapter Twenty One

He dreamed all the damned time, now. When he was awake, asleep, just lying on his back and burning up - it didn't matter none.

There were voices and flickering lights, the smell of fire, the twitch and squirm of bugs up underneath his skin, feeding on him, digging into him.

A hand landed on him, made him jerk straight upright, his groan echoing in the quiet room. "You were dreaming."

The old man had the darkest eyes. Nearly black in a load of heavy wrinkles.

"You all right now, son?" He remembered when Preacher used to call him that. Must have gotten it from the old man.

"I'm older than I look." He rasped it out, hunting a grin that he sure as Hell didn't feel, deep down.

"So am I. Think on that one, son." The old fart had a real smile for him, and a bottle of whiskey to sip from besides. "You look like you got drug under a wagon."

"I wasn't so lucky." No. He'd been dragged under a pack of starving beasts that wanted nothing more than flesh and blood and fear.

"Well, you made it through the fire, didn't you? Can I get you anything?"

When he looked around he could see Abraham sleeping by the fire, and Bear propped up against a wall, wrapped in a blanket. But not Preacher.

"Where's the padre?" He tried to stand up, tried to find his man.

"Calm down, son." Jett pushed him back down on his pallet, one hand on his shoulder. "He's fine. He's meditating on the situation."

In the dark. Things were out there in the dark.

Things like him.

"Where?"

"He's safe, son. This is my place. Won't no one come here. Nothing bad, leastways." Those eyes stared right into him, seeing too damned much, he'd bet.

He was there. "You know who was hunting us?"

Hunting him.

Hunting Fred.

"I do." Dead certain, that was what the man was. Calm, for all that, but dead certain.

"I'm going to kill him." Or die trying.

If he could kill the thing, that was. He couldn't remember how, if he ever knew how.

"Well, Virgil seems set on it, too, so I guess you'll do. You gotta heal up some first." He got another sip of whiskey before Jett set the bottle aside.

He could feel the scars on his throat just a'burning and buzzing. Some stuff you just never did heal from. Ever.

"Better now, son?" Those old eyes just watched and watched. Like the man knew. Knew all about him.

"Been worse. Who are you?" There was a low-level buzzing in the base of his skull, something he ought to know but didn't.

"I'm just an old preacher, Hawk. A man of the cloth. No one you need to fear." One hand brushed his forehead, seeming to take some of the fever heat with it.

He coulda argued that men of the cloth were something he'd spent eons fearing, but that touch eased him and the argument left him in a rush.

"There, you see? You need to rest. Heal. Preacher is praying on what to do next, something he forgot for a bit. All will be well." Lord, his eyelids felt heavy.

He forced them open, staring up at the old man. "He's got his teeth set to me." The old man should know. Carchion would hunt him down.

"He does. You offended him, son. You surely did." The man sounded downright cheery. That was just. Well, Hell.

He caught himself laughing, the sound rough enough to make Dime bark in surprise and then come wagging, pink tongue hanging out. "You're crazy, mister. I like that."

"Well, you don't see all I have and stay absolutely sane." Eyes twinkling, Jett rubbed Dime's ears, making that silly mutt fall over as his good legs started thumping.

His eyes watched as long as they could before they drifted shut, the last thing he saw being Dime's shadow, leg just moving and happy.

Chapter Twenty Two

Preacher was hot as Hell, and his eyes burned from staring into the little fire he'd built.

He'd been out there in the grass for three days, praying on what they'd seen and what they'd done and what they had yet to do, and he wasn't sure he was any closer to an answer.

Damn Jett anyway for making him do this alone. Jett was a good counsel, had been ever since he'd found Preacher in a jail outside Fort Stockton waiting for a hanging of his own for shooting a man during his last bank robbery. Lord knew how Jett had talked that crusty, old sheriff out of it, sneaking him out in the middle of the night and beating him until he was sober.

He closed his eyes against the burn, really letting his mind wander now, begging for a solution. They had to find that thing that had come after them, had to keep it from Hawk. He needed Hawk, not just for himself, but for his cause. He felt it deep.

He could remember being out here like this, for blistering days and endless goddamn nights, just praying and begging for the good Lord to tell him something, to show him what to do. What he couldn't figure now was why it was taking so damned long, why he couldn't wrap his pea brain around shit.

Some things didn't change, he reckoned. He was so damned tired. Bone weary. His head drooped on his neck, almost snapping as he nodded off and then jerked awake.

Hands landed on his shoulders, heavy and hot, rubbing right off and how the Hell he knew it was Hawk, he wasn't sure, but he sure as fuck did.

Thank God. Preacher moaned, leaning into the touch. "Missed you."

"You ran off." Hawk leaned into his back, heart pounding against his spine. "Got tired of waiting."

"Yeah? You feeling better?" Reaching up, he grabbed those rough hands and pulled them down around his waist so he could pet Hawk's arms.

"I reckon to live. You find the answers you were looking for yet?"

"Not really. Just can't seem to find the answer." Maybe he needed to know more of the question. "What is he, Hawk. What does he exist for?"

"Eating." Hawk's lips were on the back of his throat, and it was all he could do not to shudder. "Some come to him and his promises, some are brought to him. Either way, he feeds on 'em 'til there ain't nothing left but a shell."

"Then we have to figure how to starve him, yeah?" That was an idea. But how?

"We'll have to kill the hounds. We... they bring him food when he's trapped away from people."

"And how do we do that?" It had to be hurting Hawk to talk about this. Preacher felt it in the stiffness of Hawk's body, and he turned, drawing Hawk up against him.

Hawk pressed close, not meeting his eyes. "They're real strong; it ain't easy. We kill each other when we get weak, tear out the throat." He could feel Hawk swallow, one of those hands at Hawk's scars, rubbing.

He bent and kissed Hawk's fingers, his scars. "Well, we can work with that, at least. Somehow."

Goddamn this whole mess. He'd do it again, though, to keep Hawk.

Hawk nodded, eyes closed tight. "Once the hounds are gone, y'all just trap him. He can't cross into hallowed ground and live."

"Not... well, Hell, maybe we ought to lure him here... Jett has this place lit up with the holy like a house afire."

"He'll come for me. I'm marked now, Padre, and he ain't pleased that one of his dogs got loose."

"Well, then our best bet is to hole up here and fight him on this ground." There. That decision was easy as breathing. He hoped Jett didn't make a liar of him by kicking them off.

Hawk nodded, hands sliding up along his spine, petting him like he was a horse. "Okay, Padre. It's a plan."

The heat and the headache went away and all he felt was Hawk. Preacher tilted his head for a kiss, lips opening so he could touch Hawk's mouth with his tongue. Hawk gave up a deep groan, the kiss sharp with whiskey and smoke and need. Oh, that could be addictive, that whiskey Hawk taste. Lord. Reaching for more, he pulled Hawk closer, trying to crawl right into the man's torn skin. Torn. Preacher tugged at Hawk's clothes, needing to see.

It was like a map, somehow, one line leading to another to another. The healing sores were white beneath the leather tan, white and pink and new, dragging his eyes along.

They were far more healed than he would have thought, and for a moment he wondered if that was Hawk's doing or Jett's. Then he stopped thinking and let himself feel, kissing Hawk harder, his lips bruising right up.

The only wound open now was that poor shoulder and his fingers brushed over it, just barely petting the rough scabs and lines where Hawk'd been ripped open.

When Hawk flinched he eased off, licking his lips. "You all right? I want... well. I think you know what I want."

"Need it, Padre. I don't know when they'll come." Hawk tugged him close, mouth hard enough to split his lips, icy eyes staring into him.

Neither of them could see like Abraham, could they? No, they needed this now, and Preacher rolled into Hawk so hard they toppled, stretching out on the dusty ground and touching each other like there was no tomorrow.

"Don't burn your toes in your fire." Hawk's fingers tore at his shirt, baring his chest for that touch.

"Huh? Oh." Right. No wonder his damned feet were hot. Preacher laughed a little, scrambling up Hawk's body to pull at Hawk's pants, those buttons popping right open for him.

Hawk's laugh felt good, the scent of male need felt even better and Preacher reckoned he'd keep both. That pretty prick felt good in his hand, slapping against his palm. He stroked it, loving the weight of it, the heat. That kind of heat didn't bother him even one little bit, not like the weather. And damned if the smell wasn't so good that Preacher had to taste, bending to lick at it.

"P...padre." Hawk grunted, boot heels scrabbling on the ground, entire body gone tight as Hawk fought to move toward his lips.

"Mmmhmm." He loved it. Loved the feel of Hawk in his mouth, of Hawk's balls under his hand. Loved Hawk.

The wind started to blow, the fire snapping behind him. Hawk's motions sped with the weather, sacs soft as velvet pushing tight against his palms.

Desperate now, he licked and sucked, needing to feel Hawk move and hear him moan and feel them together. Just in case.

Hawk grabbed him, dragged him over and around, fingers fumbling with his fly as if. Oh. Oh, save him. Those lips wrapped around his prick, the sensation matching the rhythm he had going. Lord almighty. Preacher thought he might just die, but he didn't. No, he just kept on and loved on Hawk until he couldn't breathe nor see and let Hawk love him right back.

He could feel every grain of dust, every hair on Hawk's body that brushed against him, every single inch of Hawk's tongue on his shaft. When he closed his eyes he could still see the long thighs and tight belly, and the scent of Hawk surrounded him, heavy and male. Preacher pulled hard, lips tight and tongue moving up and down Hawk's shaft.

Every thing he did, Hawk answered, the pulls, the groans, the heat surrounding him like a flame.

They rocked for a long time, both of them panting and groaning, Hawk's mouth so hot on him that Preacher just whimpered, licking and trying to breathe and... damn.

He wasn't sure which one of them came first, all he knew was one groaned and the other rocked and he was swallowing and shooting and just right there, Hawk with him.

The flavor on his tongue was like nothing else, not even the whiskey he still craved, and Preacher swallowed it down. "Lord, love. Lord."

Hawk nodded against his thigh, fingers moving from squeezing to petting. "Yeah, Padre. You know it."

Preacher turned and crawled up to kiss Hawk, making it last, making them feel it. Then he sat back and looked at the sky, watching the clouds.

"So. Now we wait."

"I reckon." Hawk sighed, nodded. "He'll come, but he'll have to feed first. We got a bit."

"Then let's make the best of it, honey." Preacher grinned, kissing Hawk hard. "While we still can."

"Yeah. Put your fire out. You can pray in the company of others."

"I've done all my praying, Hawk. Now it's time for raining Hellfire. I figure together we'll be good at that."

From the look Hawk gave him, he thought maybe he had no idea.

Chapter Twenty Three

Hawk paced, watching the night skies for hints of... something.

Anything.

They were inside, talking and eating and laughing. Preparing for Carchion to arrive.

He wouldn't be here for that.

Not one hound could survive the pack. No matter how he'd imagined it, how he'd remembered, he knew the result.

Fred wandered up, pacing with him, head heavy on his shoulder. "We don't have a choice. He'll come and come. Preacher'll manage. So will you."

Fred nudged him again, making a rude noise. Oh, that damned horse never agreed with him. Not once.

"Smartassed thing, like I don't know what I'm talking about." Shithead. Hawk was gonna miss his bony ass.

Nibbling on him, Fred pulled at his shirt, hauling him back toward Jett's cabin, trying to get him within sight of Preacher, he'd bet. Damned mule.

"You are a stubborn cuss." He stumbled over a rock, bumped hard against Fred, who stumbled out of the way just in time for him to land on Preacher, who'd obviously come outside to smoke.

"Hey."

"Well, howdy. You just being unsociable?" Preacher pulled out the tobacco bag that held Bear's pre-rolled smokes, offering him one.

"Just thinking." He took one, hunting his pockets for matches. Just waiting.

"That's a dangerous proposition, honey. That thinking." A Lucifer match flared in the darkness, Preacher lighting up.

He chuckled, leaned forward to light his own off the flame. "What all do y'all got going in there?"

"Oh, Jett's got Bear making some crazy pie, and Abraham is telling stories on me." A deep inhale lit up the night, Preacher's face appearing through the smoke.

"I oughta go listen." He wondered whether they'd tell stories on him, after, if there were any of them left to tell stories at all.

"You think? Anything out in the night?" Hat tipping back, Preacher studied the night sky, just as he had.

"Not yet." Soon. It would be soon, his throat burned.

"Then we wait." In and out, Preacher pulled at his cheroot, then blew out smoke. "You worried some?"

He chewed on the end of his smoke,
thinking on that. "Just want to know y'all will
be right at the end."

"We all? You leaving us?" He could hear
the sudden tension in Preacher's voice, see the
way the cheroot quivered.

"I won't ride from here, Padre." He'd leave,
but it wouldn't be like that. No sir.

"I need you at my back, Hawk. I need you
here." One hand settled on his shoulder, just
like those first few nights, when Preacher had
made him feel so welcome.

He nodded. "You'll have all of me,
Preacher. Everything I got, you got my word."

"Then I'm the luckiest man on earth."

Thunder cracked just as they moved toward
each other, ready to grab and hold on, stopping
anything else they might have said.

"You'd best get inside, Padre. They'll be
coming." The hair on his arms was standing
straight up, vibrating.

"They will. I'm with you." That was that.
Preacher squared off with him, Fred dancing
behind them.

Hawk looked at Preacher, just staring a
second. "You ain't never fought a Hellhound."

"So? You told me how to take them. I'm not
letting you go it alone." Damn it, the man was
stubborn as the day was long.

"You. I. Damn it. They'll kill you." They
were gonna kill him, weren't they?

"Not if we all fight together." That came from behind them, the old man coming out and taking up a stand beside them. "Not if we believe we can win."

"You have to be safe for the big fight. You... You're good men, now. He can't call you." Hawk didn't know whether Carchion could call for him now. He didn't want to know.

"You are. too," Preacher said, sounding so sure. So certain. Like he could just wash away what all he'd done.

"I ain't, Padre." He turned, stared into those eyes and tried to make the man understand. "It was one little girl, Padre. One little girl that I couldn't let him have. It weren't that I turned from him, turned to your god. I just. She was *good* and I couldn't let him ruin her."

Hannah. Her name'd been Hannah.

"All it takes is one." Preacher put both hands on his shoulders, eyes so dark they looked like holes in the snow. "All it took for me was the wanting, and there was Jett. I sat in that jail and thought, 'I wish I hadn't killed that feller', and I was saved." Those hands dug into his tight muscles, easing him some. "That's all it takes."

"You can't save a monster." And that was it, wasn't it? He knew, once he died, there was nothing but fire awaiting him. Fire and Carchion's rage.

Jett snorted, the sound loud and rude. "I am a man of God, Hawk. My house is a church. You couldn't have spent three days in there with me dosing you if you weren't saved already. Now stop your whining and get ready to fight."

Lightining crashed, so bright they could all see what waited for them, dozens of glowing eyes, just beyond the ring of light, just out of range in the dark.

Hawk growled, muscles tensing as he stared into those eyes. The howling started, low and deep and he answered, his own voice threatening. His place. His family. His pack.

He would not allow them to hunt here.

Fred whinnied, hooves flashing, and even old Abraham's donkey brayed like they was backing him up. Preacher stood beside him, a light shining as big as the sun, one that would always call him home.

His nose twitched, the scents strong and sudden, crawling under his skin. He knew those smells, what they meant. Another series of howls split the air.

We're coming for you, Aquilon. You belong to us.

He threw his head back and howled. He belonged here. With Preacher. Here.

The other hounds snarled, snapped, and finally ran at them, howling in an unearthly concert. The sound of pounding feet drowned out the sharp rasp of their breathing.

He ran to meet them, teeth snapping at the air, hands that wouldn't become paws tearing and being torn. Fred was beside him, hooves flashing, the horses screams near human, sounding almost like his name.

He could hear shouts, see flashing blades as Preacher and Jett fought beside him. And he'd be damned if he didn't see one hound go down with an arrow in its throat. Looked like Bear had joined the fight.

The smell of blood sent them into a rage and he watched it, waiting for the madness to take him and shake him. It didn't, but the big alpha sure as shit did, headbutting him and sending him reeling.

The sharp teeth closed over his wrist and he screamed, thumb pushing into one eye, pressing until he heard a pop, a howl, felt those teeth biting deeper.

Fred screamed too, that sound that only a mad horse could produce, bounding into the fray to kick the shit out of that hound, slicing it on the other side of its face. Hawk called out, grabbed for that mane as soon as the beast let him go. Fred yanked him up, pulling him out of the way of those teeth.

Something flashed off to his right, the dying gurgle of a hound loud as could be, even over all of the barking and snapping. Red eyes glowed, the smell of brimstone awful, singeing his nose.

Something bloomed in his chest, something close to hope. His foot lashed out at the next beast that came for them, catching it in the throat with a bone-rattling thud.

It wasn't easy. God knew he was bleeding from a thousand tiny cuts, but it seemed almost like they were pushing the hounds back. Hell, he could swear he even saw Abraham out there, waving a cane around and around, shouting about the light brigade...

He will take you back in, Aquilon. He will allow you to come home, to run with the pack. The words echoed in his head, clear as a bell. A smaller hound stood before him, staring at him. *Come back. We will follow you again.*

Fred reared, near unseating him, but it was Preacher who darted in under Fred's flashing hooves and went right for that damned hound's throat.

"I will not, Carchion! Do you hear me?" His voice sounded too loud to his own ears, echoing louder than the thunder.

The storm answered him, the flash of lightning slamming into the ground, blinding him.

"No! You will not have him!" Like a madman, Preacher fought for him, kicking and punching and swinging what looked like a scythe when his vision cleared.

He leapt down, fighting beside his padre, refusing to back away, to back down. Finally the last hound fell, trampled into an unrecognizable mass in the mud.

They survived.

They had survived.

"Congratulations, Aquilon. You led your little band into a fight with dogs. How incredibly charming."

An terrible weight drove him to his knees, Carchion standing at the edge of the clearing, smiling over the destruction.

Preacher knelt beside him, bloody hands clamping down on his arms. "Don't you listen to him, Hawk. We made our stand. We won. He can't hurt us here or he already would have."

"Will he be the first one you bring me, dog? It would be nothing, to rip that soul we gave you away. Wouldn't it be lovely, to hear him jibbering and pleading while you pant at my feet?"

Hawk growled, the familiar rage sparking at Carchion's words.

Turning his face with a hand on either cheek, Preacher looked right into his eyes, staring until all he could see was how much that man needed him. "Stay with me, Hawk. We can beat him."

"I told you, Padre. I ain't leaving this place without you." Whatever Hannah'd give him, whatever spark that little girl lit, it weren't nothing Carchion could give or take away. That was the goddamn lie.

It always had been.

"There you go." Preacher kissed him, right there in front of God and everybody, not long nor hard nor nothin', just sweet and good, and then the man stood, facing Carchion and tugging at Hawk's arm and he followed.

"Come and get us, you bastard, if you can."

Carchion's eyes blazed, the heat reaching across the way. Hawk laughed, the sound rolling out of him like thunder. That was his man. His own.

"On your knees, Aquilon!"

"My name is Hawk." And he wasn't going to kneel for that son of a bitch again.

"You are not welcome here!" Jett's voice broke out, louder than thunder, stronger than Hellfire. "You dare not come on this ground!"

"I'll leave, once you give me what belongs to me." Those eyes landed on him, his blood hot enough to boil. "I will spare them, but you are mine."

He could see it, sudden and sharp, Bear scalped and Abraham slit open. His dear Fred broken and hurting, legs shattered. Worst of all, Preacher, drowning in pain.

"You'll have to try and take him, because he's with us now. 'Course you ain't got the balls the Lord gave a donkey," Preacher said, driving the image away. The braying of Abraham's donkey in the silence after made him smile.

He stepped back toward the cabin, putting space between him and Preacher.

Carchion smiled and the look chilled him like icy water. Those teeth were sharp, shining like chips of glass in the sunshine. "Come take me, dog. Prove your god will protect you.."

"He already did, you stupid bastard, else I'd be a damned man and you'd be celebrating." Hawk didn't falter, didn't sway. He just stood and looked into the eyes of Hell itself, screaming out. "Now! You. Come. Take. Me."

His voice made the ground shake.

Pacing back and forth along the mouth of the clearing, Carchion growled, the sound creating a wind that blew bits of fur and blood past him. "Aquilon. You will turn on him someday. Just as you did me."

"He never once had to hobble me to keep me."

"Do you think his god approves?" Carchion thundered, and lightning split the sky, throwing off sparks that set little patches of grass to burning.

A pure white fury lit in him and he stepped forward, shaking with it. "What do you know of it? You and I come from the same goddamn fires, you piece of shit. You think you can take me? Quit acting like a yellow-bellied coward and come prove it!"

Preacher stood with him, whether he wanted the man to or not, and goddamned if that man didn't pick up a rock and hurl it at the demon that stood screaming at them. "Come on, ya bastard!"

Carchion growled, hand wrapping around the stone and crushing it to dust, the bits of ash smoking and burning as they fell to the ground.

"Do you even begin, child, to think you can best me?" Those eyes fell on Preacher, the glow familiar. "You are a drunk and a lout. You follow your god out of fear that what you believe is true. That you are damned."

Oh, now. This was just enough. Hawk caught sight of Fred, moving around the back of the demon, ready to strike. Before Carchion could notice, he ran forward into those burning arms, pulling as Fred pushed the bastard forward onto hallowed ground.

He felt the burn, saw the flames light up all around him, and he laughed, leaning up to growl into the demon's ear. "I was blind, but now I see."

Chapter Twenty Four

Preacher stood for long moments and stared. Hawk...Oh, Lord, he was gonna lose Hawk. Wasn't no way he could walk through that fire, not as much of a sinner as he was. That... that thing. It was right. He only believed out of fear.

While he dithered, things were happening fast. Bear was burning up hound bodies, and Abraham was crying and Jett was putting Fred's nose hairs out where they was on fire.

He reached in to get Hawk and drew back with a shout, his hand blistering right up. Goddamn it, why was he faltering now?

Coal-red eyes caught his, burning into his skull. *You failed him. You gave him to me.*

No! He wailed it inside, but it wouldn't come out of his mouth. It just wouldn't. His hands clenched and unclenched and he watched Hawk writhe and he couldn't even get out a goddamned prayer.

Yes. He'll burn, twist for me for an eternity. The demon's flesh bubbled, beginning to melt.

Hawk didn't deserve to burn because of him. No sir. Preacher steeled himself, rushing right into the fire to pull Hawk away. He'd go down first.

Hawk was right there, stretching for him, hands open and reaching, the demon forgotten. Those lips were moving, no sounds coming out at all, but Preacher knew Hawk was praying for him.

Oh. Oh, God. Preacher reached right out and grabbed Hawk's hand, feeling the rough skin, the real warmth of Hawk's flesh, not the heat from a false fire.

Hawk's fingers gripped him, holding on tight and he tugged, the long body coming easy.

No. No! You can't HAVE him!

Hawk's eyes were laughing.

Laughing.

He'd be damned.

"You son of a bitch! I got you now!" Jett came flying past them, looking like some kind of demented avenging angel, Bible in one hand, a shiny silver blade in the other. He and Hawk tumbled to the ground, out of the flames, both of them watching with wide eyes.

The demon screamed, launching himself at Jett and... the damned horse?

Fred's hooves flashed, the beast fighting alongside Jett like he belonged here.

Preacher scrambled back, watching Jett and Fred slash and poke at the damned demon who seemed to be melting and then flaring back up, kinda like Bear's beans in a pot. It beat all he ever did see, but none of it seemed to scare him, not with Hawk holding onto him.

Jett's arm flashed down, knife sliding into that damned demon, sinking deep and the cursed thing growled, falling to its knees. He felt a flare of hope when the burning eyes closed, praise God, but then the old man's head snapped back, blood bubbling from his lips as a hand – a whole hand, appeared from behind, clawed fingers opening and closing.

Jesus, no.

Hawk launched himself forward without a sound and slapped up against Bear. Those big hands came up, started dragging them both away from the fray, tears streaking the dark cheeks. Preacher retched, sliding on the mud as Fred screamed, a pure agony in the sound.

Another flash of lightning flared and for a second – just a heartbeat – Preacher didn't see hooves and tail and mane. He saw a man, driving the demon deep into the ground.

Jett screamed, the sound triumphant, and followed the demon down, silver blade stabbing down, and the fire exploded out like a shooting star, blinding him completely. All Preacher could hear was Bear grunting and Hawk shouting something, and the crackle of the whole world burning.

The world came back to him in bits and pieces, Jett's bed soft underneath him.

"Hawk?" He always came back to Hawk, feeling like that man was his real salvation.

"He's outside with the horses, I'm afraid. He and Bear are destroying the bodies." Abraham stood over him, pale as milk. "I'm sorry, friend, but your mentor was lost."

"My..." He rose up on one elbow, listening to his bones creak. He felt as old as the hills. "Jett?" he asked hoarsely, clenching his burnt hand just to feel it hurt.

Abraham nodded, tears on the doughy cheeks. "He drove the beast into the ground, but he... I'm sorry."

"He what?" Clutching at Abraham's shirt front, Preacher snarled. "He what, goddamnit. Speak up like a man for once in your measly life."

"He fell. He's gone. There is nothing left but this." Abraham picked up a blackened blade, pressed it into his hands.

Fell. Fell where? Into what? Did that demon suck his old friend into Hell? God almighty, he hurt. Preacher fell back, staring at the ceiling. "Sorry, Abe. Didn't mean to hurt."

"I understand, friend. I do." Abraham sighed, moved away to the window, staring out into the growing light.

Had it only been one night?

"How long?" Clearing his throat, Preacher tried again. "How long have I been out?"

"A few hours, I believe. Bear and Hawk brought you in. I think they wanted me to stay."

"I bet. Turn your stomach for sure and none of us could breathe then." Feeling churlish, he looked Abraham over. "You all still there?"

"I believe I am. I. I believe that Bear and I came out of this hurt least of all."

"What about Dime? And Fred?" He wanted to drag his sorry ass out of the bed and see, go find Hawk, but every time he tried he just fell back. His body felt broke as Hell somehow.

"The pup is fine. Hawk would not allow anyone near the horse." Abraham looked at him, eyes wide. "He *shot* at me to make his point known."

"Who did?" What the Hell? "Is Fred all right? Do we have any horses left? I'm sorry about your donkey."

"I haven't the foggiest idea, man. Your paramour shot at me. I did not remain outside to argue with him." Abraham almost looked het up. Preacher was damn near impressed.

"Well, help me up, will you?" What in the name of all that was holy was wrong with him? His legs felt like a newborn colt's.

Abraham helped him move toward the door, his bare feet scraping on the hard-pack. Damn, they'd took his boots off, too?

Leaning on the doorjamb, he looked out, seeing Jett's land burned right down to the soil, great rents in the ground showing where lightning had hit. "The lean-to and house made it... Lord, lord."

Bear was stoking a massive fire and Hawk was walking Fred, slow and steady, refusing to let the horse lie down.

It looked like there'd been a war, not just a one-night battle.

"Where's my boots, Abraham? I'll go and help." He saw his hat, hanging on the other side of the door, looking about like it had the day Jett had given it to him.

"Are you quite sure? You look like you could use another rest, honestly."

"Damn it, man, don't treat me like a baby!" He growled it out, just slapping his hand against the wall next to the door. "I need to *do* something. Jett's dead and it's all my fault and I got to..." he hung his head, breathing hard. "I got to help make it right."

"He went rejoicing. It was his calling, to fight that demon. You assisted him in his life's work." Abraham handed him his boots, not backing away from his temper at all.

Raising a brow, Preacher yanked on one boot, then another, biting back his groans. "Rejoicing. You betcha."

Clapping his hat on his head, he stomped out into the clearing, taking it all in.

It was oddly silent, neither Bear nor Hawk saying a damn word. All he heard was the wind, the slap of Fred's hooves in the mud and the crackle of the fire.

It felt like an accusation, and he didn't blame them at all. Preacher went to Bear first, clapping the man on the shoulder. "You all right, Bear? Anything I can do?"

Bear looked him over, then tugged him into a tight, quick hug, hands slapping his back. Then he was turned toward Hawk and sorta shoved.

Hard.

Preacher stumbled, hands out to try and right himself, and he went right into Hawk's back, both of them grunting. "Hey, Mister. You need some help with Fred?"

Hawk nodded to him, mouth moving, nothing but air coming through. Those blood-shot blue eyes rolled, and he got a wry grin, then they started walking again.

Preacher grinned a little, easing in his bones when he realized Hawk's silence was a sore throat and not anger. Then he ducked to Fred's opposite side, helping pull the silly nag along.

There were some deep cuts in Fred's side, scratches that had to hurt, but it was the dropped head, the listless motions that worried him.

"Is he hurt inside?" He patted Fred on the neck, just feeling dread in his gut. If Fred died, Hawk might never forgive him.

Hawk shrugged, mouthing 'not his body'. One hand reached out for him, under Fred's jaw.

He took it, holding on. Oh. Better. "Well, we just need to get him a filly or something." It was weak, but it was an attempt.

Hawk chuckled, the action soundless, but amused nonetheless.

Yeah. Something.

Preacher sighed. Well, now what? They'd beaten back the night, but at what cost? He sure didn't know what to do from there.

Hawk stopped all of a sudden like, looked at him and tugged him around for a deep, hard kiss.

Oh.

Oh, damnation, he could live for this alone. Preacher put his arms around Hawk's back and kissed back, needing the flavor and feel of it.

The kiss went deep, Hawk tasting him and bringing him right back to the middle, hand on his neck to steady him. When their lips parted, they swayed, both of them groaning.

"Thought I'd lost you," he said, hands clenching on Hawk's arms. "Scared me half to death."

"Told...told you. Not leaving without you." The words were just whispered, the sounds pained.

"You did." He stroked Hawk's cheek, finally beginning to believe. Finally. "I trust you, Hawk. With my life."

Hawk nodded, starting them walking again like it was normal as sunrise, like this morning was just another day.

And Hell. Maybe it was.

The first day of their new life and their new mission.

Chapter Twenty Five

Three days after things went to Hell and his voice still hadn't come back.

His breath came easy and his dreams had turned to riding and roping, to snow and mountains and all.

To moving on.

It weren't that he didn't like it here, it was more that he wasn't the type of man to stay in one spot. He reckoned Abraham liked it, the way the man was setting up house and all; but him and Bear was looking to the horizon.

That just left Preacher.

Hawk headed out of the barn, thinking on how to tell that stubborn sky pilot what was in his head.

Preacher was out working in the sun, his coat and hat on a rock, that graying head shining in the light. The man seemed to think it was his mission to put the ground to rights where Jett had gone down, working on it with a dogged determination.

Hawk was sure that Preacher could dig and fuss and all for a month of Sundays and not make a difference.

Jett was gone, at least the body was.

He stood and watched, waiting for Preacher to see his shadow.

The man finally looked up, those stormcloud eyes dark and tired, but Preacher had a smile for him, as usual. "Hey, mister."

He nodded, grinned. Time to ride. The mountains were calling. He held out one hand to Preacher.

Preacher came to him immediately, hand sliding into his. "How's the throat?"

He opened his mouth, but stopped before he tried to speak and shrugged instead.

"Uh huh. Well, I sure do miss your voice." There was a wry humor to that, one of Preacher's eyebrows waggling. "How's Fred?"

Ready to go. Ready to run. Looking for something.

Hawk reached out, tugged Preacher close for a kiss. Fred would be fine.

Humming, Preacher kissed him right back, arms closing around him. This he'd miss. The freedom to do this whenever he wanted to.

A deep groan left him, surprising him as the sound pushed into Preacher's lips. An answering moan came from Preacher and they locked together, both of them pressing the kiss harder and harder. Both of them needy.

His. They knelt together, swaying a little as they got balanced on their knees. The kisses healed him up. Always had. He knew it, down at the river, Preacher's touch on his throat. His seemed to give Preacher strength. The man seemed ready to just eat him up, ready to crawl inside him, urgent and hotter than the sun up in the sky.

Hawk wrapped around the man like paper around tobacco, holding on tight. He reckoned he'd been saved from what he'd been, that worry just slipping away. Preacher tipped his head back and kissed his throat, like the man was bent on healing it, licking and nibbling everywhere.

"P...padre." The words scraped out of him like diamonds over glass.

"Uh huh." Loving him, Preacher moved down the scars on his shoulder, his shirt just slipping right off.

It made his head toss, to be bare under the sun, to be able to touch and feel under the bright sky.

They had all day, but Preacher was in a hurry anyway, stripping him down, pushing his dungarees down...

His prick reached right up for that touch, wanting nothing more than Preacher's attention, craving it like a drunk craved the burn of whiskey.

"I can smell you, Hawk." Preacher pulled back, licking his lips like a starving man. "Let me taste you?"

"Anything." He liked to whimpered, arching back toward the ground, cock slapping his belly.

"Now." Diving right down his body, Preacher tasted him, tongue running right along the length of his prick like it was the medicine Preacher needed to heal him.

His thighs went tight as bow strings, hips rocking up, pushing and begging for that sweet, hot mouth.

Giving him everything seemed to come easy to Preacher, and the man swallowed him right down, tongue working the underside. Strong hands cupped his bottom, lifting him right up, helping him stay up where Preacher could rock him, make him crazy.

It was all he needed, all he wanted, to push close and press into that heat. Words started coming - all those words that had been caught up in his throat just pouring down over Preacher's head. Nodding along, Preacher gave him just what he wanted, what he craved, sucking hard. One rough hand slid down to cup his balls, rolling them.

His climax tumbled right down his spine and then through his cock, seed spurting from him as he howled out his pleasure.

The padre took him right down, licking him clean, taking every drop he had to give. Then Preacher all but bowled him over rising up to kiss him.

He took that kiss, wrapping right around Preacher, arms and legs. Grunting, Preacher humped against him, cock settling against his hips through the wool pants Preacher still had on.

He reached down, fighting desperately to get to skin, to feel Preacher's heat against him. The man moved into his touch and those buttons popped all over, flying through the air, and finally Preacher was naked against him, cock hot and damp, sliding along his skin. Preacher groaned like a man in pain, rocking hard on him.

His hand curled around Preacher's hip, pulling the man closer, tugging hard.

It took maybe another two, maybe three thrusts before Preacher called his name, voice soaring right up to startle the birds. Hot seed landed on his skin, making him moan.

Their lips met again, both of them blinking and staring.

And smiling.

Smiling like two newborn fools.

Preacher kissed him one more time before stroking his cheek and nodding. "Time to move on, huh?"

"Yeah. Yeah, I reckon. You done your job."

"Then let's ride, Hawk. I can almost feel Jett on the wind, telling us to move on. Abraham agrees."

"I'll be with you." Right where he belonged, whether or not anyone approved.

"You said you'd ride with me, by my side. I trust you to stay."

That was all he needed to hear.

It was time to go. Together.

Epilogue

Goddamn, he needed to get himself a church.

Oh, Preacher knew that wasn't his mission. He needed to be a traveling man, but it still hurt his ass.

He glanced over at Hawk and Bear, who were tearing down the tent and packing up the mules. Abraham had stayed behind at Jett's homestead, claiming they needed a home base, and while Preacher missed the man's face once in awhile, he sure didn't miss the farting.

Rubbing the back of his neck, Preacher wandered over, the dust of the town feeling gritty on his hands and face.

"Y'all gonna be chapped at me if we move on this afternoon? I want to get out and get away from the prying eyes."

Hawk's icy blue eyes laughed at him from under that big, old hat brim. "You got enough of their pennies and souls, Padre?"

"I do. I'm ready to move on." They'd saved a few souls. He knew it deep in his bones. That was enough for him.

"Well, then. Get your bony ass up on that horse."

Bear laughed at them, the sound weird and rough, but a sound, nonetheless. A laugh.

His old gelding was gone, lost not long after the fight at Jett's. He had a brand new mount, a big, rawboned dapple gray that acted a hellacious lot like Fred. "Soon as y'all get packed I will. I swear that horse has the roughest gait I ever did feel."

"He's got some spirit to him, sure enough." Hawk looked like he knew something there for a second, eyes sharp and bright for just a heartbeat, then it faded away.

Sorta like Hawk's memory of all the stuff that'd happened to them. Sometimes the man would dream, but mostly? It was just gone.

"He does." Fred had perked up since the cussed thing had shown up, too, so Preacher couldn't complain.

That apple-headed critter nudged him good and hard, almost like it was poking at him. Fred, the old shit, just stamped and whinnied, making Hawk shake his head.

"Come on, sky pilot. We need to feel the wind. Bear's got bacon for supper."

"We can even have beans." Grinning, he mounted up while Bear tightened the last strap on the packs. The big gray danced under him, making him cuss and clutch at his hat.

"Don't fall now." Hawk swung up into Fred's saddle, those dungarees pulling tight over the man's hind end making it look...

Damn.

They left the town behind in short order, all of them making tracks. It was just harder to be among folks after all they'd seen and done. After all they knew. He kicked his mount into a lope and let him run, hearing Hawk whoop behind him.

It felt damn fine, to let the horses have their heads, to head northwest toward the mountains that Hawk kept muttering about. The wind was crisp and cool, and he didn't reckon they'd get to where they were going 'til the spring rains, but that was okay.

They slowed, finally, Bear searching the horizon for a place to camp, Dime barking his fool head off, and him and Hawk riding side-by-side, just like he figured they ought.

He could hear water running, just burbling and dancing somewhere close and he'd be damned if Hawk didn't grin over, nod once. "I'll fetch us water for the night."

"Bear, you need anything?"

When the stocky half-breed shook his head, Preacher grinned himself. "I'll help."

"Yeah. Come on then." Fred tossed his head as Hawk kicked him and off they went, dust just a'flyin'.

Preacher took off after, suddenly feeling years younger. They rode until the horses took over, barreling toward the water.

Hawk pulled up, Fred coming up just short of the water, hooves actually splashing a little as Hawk hooted.

Preacher almost went ass over teakettle when his horse stopped, and he patted the big old monster's neck. "What do you figure I ought to name him?"

Hawk tilted his head, thinking on it. "He's a fierce 'un. What was your Jett's family name?"

"Cain. Now that would be a good name for him." He patted the silly nag's neck, ground tying him and letting him graze.

"There you go." Hawk pulled the water jugs down before stripping his jacket and shirtsleeves off, heading straight off to wash in the cold water.

Watching, Preacher admired the lean lines of that body, that man he'd fought so hard to save. Lord, he did love that feller.

"Damn. It's cold as a well digger's butt." Hawk splashed a little more on himself, then stood up, letting Preacher see that long, lean body.

He moved toward the stream, drawn like a bee to honey. "Yeah? Sounds good after all the dust." His long, black coat hit the dirt on the bank.

"It's sweet as all get out." The drops of water hung from that mustache, Hawk licking them away.

Preacher pushed right on into the water, gasping as it rose above his boots. He pulled his shirt off and tossed it aside, too, before splashing himself. "Shitfire."

Hawk chuckled, hat going to sit atop their clothes. "Makes your balls crawl up, don't it?"

"It does. Good thing I got you to warm me up." He grinned back like a newborn fool, rubbing his arms.

"I reckon." Hawk leaned forward, licked some water off one shoulder before backing away.

Glancing up, he caught Hawk staring, chuckling, and Preacher scooped up a palmful of water, slinging it right at Hawk, his aim sure and true.

Hawk sputtered and growled, pouncing him, their skin slapping together before they slipped, going ass over teakettle into the river with a splash.

Cold.

Cold.

They came up gasping and cussing, slogging up on the bank together. Hawk's body was firm, hard against him, and Preacher let himself lean a little when they sat, watching the puffy, little clouds overhead.

His hand landed in Hawk's lap and he'd be damned if Hawk didn't lean in, whisper low. "You best watch it, Padre. I hear I'm trouble."

"I've heard that about you. Good thing it's my job to borrow trouble, huh?" God, he loved it when Hawk laughed. It wasn't near as rare a thing as it had once been.

"Damn good." Hawk hauled him close, brought their lips together in a kiss that liked to set him afire, balls to bones.

The cold water was just a memory by the time that kiss ended, and when they finished the second one his hand was doing more than just sitting there. Yes sir, it was a busy old hand, pushing against Hawk's crotch.

Hawk groaned into his lips, that heavy shaft pushing and throbbing and begging for more of him. "Padre. I got a need."

"I can feel, Hawk. I surely can." His fingers worked at Hawk's buttons, a little stiff from the cold, but getting there anyway. Once he had that fly open, Preacher dug right in, groaning when Hawk's prick pushed against his palm.

He got himself a moan and an arch and those hands just grabbed at him, keeping him close. That mustache rasped at his skin as Hawk's mouth moved over his face, his jaw.

Tilting his head back, he let Hawk taste his fill, reaching his other hand down to cup and squeeze. He loved how hot and silky Hawk's cock felt after a day of rough and grit and riding.

That hungry mouth moved down his throat toward his chest and, as it did, they rolled down into the grass, side-by-side. He kissed Hawk then, his mouth open so he could bring Hawk to taste him, taste his need. Their tongues pushed together, sliding and slipping and God help him but his Hawk stole his breath clean away.

They moved closer together, his hand never stopping its slow movement, pulling at Hawk's hard flesh. A man could die for this. He surely could.

Hawk's hips rolled, pushing into his hand over and over, the deep moans coming faster and faster as Hawk tried to speed him along.

"Hungry. You're damned hungry." Not that he wasn't a greedy bastard, because he was. It was his turn to lick and kiss down a sweet expanse of skin, and he touched his lips to Hawk's throat, just like he always did.

And just like always, Hawk lifted his chin, asking for more. Even those hips slowed their rocking as Hawk moaned for him, focused on his lips. Preacher licked over every scar, kissed every piece of raised flesh. He thanked God every day Hawk had been too strong to break.

"Padre." Hawk held him close, that voice strong, sure. "I got a need of you."

His whole body surged. Surely Hawk didn't mean. Hell, even he hadn't done that more'n once or twice. "Want me in you?"

"Hmm?" Hawk moaned again, nodding once as they rubbed together. "Need you, Preacher. However."

Oh, merciful heavens. His cock surged, and Preacher wiggled back to get them both stripped off, making time. He'd not thought to do that, had never even dared, but oh...

Hawk was hard as stone, tip wet and leaking from wanting him and Lord, he could smell Hawk's need. Hawk helped him with his own kit, fingers sliding over his skin, just stroking away.

His hands shook over the last few scraps, and he kissed Hawk good and hard just to steady his nerves, sinking into the wild taste. His Hawk gave as good as he got, lips wrapped around his tongue, sucking nice and hard.

He touched Hawk all over, hands sliding down that strong back to cup Hawk's buttocks, testing the muscles there, squeezing. Lord, he might just explode. That pretty backside was tight as a boar's, but Hawk spread like soft butter when his hands asked it, pushing one leg to the side.

His fingers traced Hawk's mouth when he pulled back from the kiss, his thumb pushing down, opening Hawk up for him. Those winter-sky blue eyes widened, but Hawk let him in, let him touch, the heat between them steady as anything.

Nodding, holding that gaze, Preacher slipped two fingers into Hawk's mouth, encouraging him with a moan. "That's it. Feels good, lover."

Hawk sucked him right in, tongue sliding over his fingertips. Now that made lightning shoot down his spine. Damn.

Panting, he held on as long as he could, that touch making him think of wicked things a man ought not do in daylight, out in the open. Then Preacher pulled his fingers free and reached behind Hawk, trying to push real gentle like.

Hawk's shoulders left the grass, mouth crashing into his as he spread that little, secret entrance. Tight. Tight. Lord help him, that was gonna feel like.

Oh.

His fingers slipped in, opened that hidden hole, and Preacher felt his eyes roll like those of a fractious pony. He was never gonna last.

"Padre." Hawk gasped his name out, hands gripping at his arms as that ring of muscles squeezed him tight as all get out.

"Breathe for me, Hawk. Just breathe and relax." He could say that to himself, too. So he did just that, letting air swell in his lungs. Then he moved his fingers again, spreading them wider.

Hawk's chest rose, then that tight body eased for him, just enough to let him push deeper, touch his Hawk. Preacher got lost in it for long moments, pushing in and out, loving the heat and tightness, the way Hawk bucked when he hit something small and firm inside.

"Please. Again." Hawk's eyes flared, the heat and hunger in them bigger than the both of them.

"There?" Oh, right there. Hawk went crazy for him, and Preacher wanted that again and again. Almost as much as he wanted inside.

Those strong, callused hands framed his face, Hawk's kiss sloppy and frantic. "Need. *Need.*"

"Yes. Now." He pulled his fingers free and wet himself down with spit in his palm. Then he pushed Hawk over on his back, muscling up between those strong thighs, his cock pressing where his fingers had been.

"Ready?"

"Yes. Now." He was drawn in, Hawk's hands moving him close. He slipped in, cock wrapped in incredible heat.

His head was going to explode. Simply fly away. Preacher pushed into Hawk, hand on those hips, pulling him up to meet each thrust. There wasn't anything else so good. Anything so right than the way Hawk's body clung to him.

"Padre. Preacher." His name rang out, echoing against the stones like a hymn.

He'd found his home, no matter where he was. Letting the need take him, Preacher pressed into Hawk. In, then out, their skin rubbing, Hawk's muscles pulling at him. His breath sawed in his chest, his hips rocking faster and faster.

A flush crawled its way up Hawk's body, telling him that Hawk was fixin' to tumble over into pleasure. All he could do was grab Hawk's prick and pull, wanting them to go together like they did in everything else.

The tight sheath around his prick rippled, squeezed tight, and then heat poured over his fingers, the scent of Hawk hitting his nose.

"Hawk!" Preacher called out his lover's name, came inside him, and the world stood still for a moment, even the birds and the stream fading away. All he could feel was Hawk, and how damned much he loved this man.

Hawk held him close, refusing to let him go. Their lips came together, Hawk's tongue sliding in to taste him.

The kiss went on and on, both of them licking and humming, hands moving slowly on sweaty skin. Preacher nuzzled his way down to Hawk's throat, needing to press his mouth there, loving on those scars, old and new.

Hawk moaned for him, throat working as he licked, healed. Gave Hawk something no one else could.

"Glad you're with me, Hawk. Always glad." He kissed Hawk's mouth again, smiling down into those shining eyes. There wasn't even a hint of a cloud in the sky. Not one bit of a storm.

"You won't be riding alone again, Padre." That? Was a prayer if he'd ever heard one.

End

BA Tortuga

Printed in the United States
88828LV00001B/14/A

9 781934 166444